# The Tyrant

# The Tyrant

## A North-Western Story

# MAX BRAND™

**Thorndike Press • Chivers Press**
**Waterville, Maine USA   Bath, England**

This Large Print edition is published by Thorndike Press, USA and by Chivers Press, England.

Published in 2002 in the U.S. by arrangement with Golden West Literary Agency.

Published in 2002 in the U.K. by arrangement with Golden West Literary Agency.

U.S.  Hardcover 0-7838-9129-6   (Western Series)
U.K.  Hardcover 0-7540-4973-6   (Chivers Large Print)
U.K.  Softcover  0-7540-4974-4   (Camden Large Print)

The text of this Large Print edition is unabridged.
Other aspects of the book may vary from the original edition.

Cover design by Thorndike Press Staff.

Set in 16 pt. Plantin.

Printed in the United States on permanent paper.

**British Library Cataloguing-in-Publication Data available**

**Library of Congress Cataloging-in-Publication Data**

Brand, Max, 1892–1944.
     The tyrant : a north-western story / Max Brand.
        p.   cm.
     ISBN 0-7838-9129-6  (lg. print : hc : alk. paper)
     1. Trappers — Fiction.   2. Canada — Fiction.
  3. Large type books.   I. Title.
  PS3511.A87 T9 2002
     813'.52—dc21                                    2001051768

# THE TYRANT

## A North-Western Story

# Chapter One

# The Forest Man

It is the misfortune of most, in beginning their memoirs, that they are forced to write down many first recollections that have nothing to do with the long tenor of the lives that followed. In this respect, I am lucky. The first thing I could remember was the weird singing from the Limousin River as the trappers followed the current with rhythmic dippings of their paddles. Once, when I heard that song from the heart of the night, I awakened and crept to the window and looked out. Through a cleft among the big evergreens that stood between our house and the water, I saw two long canoes, each manned by four paddlers, shoot like two strange shadows across the moon-silvered river.

They were racing for the town, and I knew that the odd mounds of blackness in the center of each canoe consisted of precious furs brought out of the great cold wilderness that extended north and west — north and west to the end of the world. It was a prophecy that my own steps were to turn in that direction.

This was my first memory. The second was far more vivid. Although I was to see so much of the man afterward, the impression that his hideous face made on me that first day was never quite the same.

I was five years old, and the whole event stands in the shadows of my childhood like a bright Italian painting in a dim room. It was a white, still day, so cold that my nurse said even the wind dared not stir. My mother was afraid to let me go out into such weather, but my stern father laughed at her, saying: "He is not a boy . . . he is a man!"

"Alas, alas," said my poor mother, "is he a man so soon?"

She gave up at once, as she always did, and my father, in person, bustled me out of the house, telling the nurse not to treat me as though I would break. I was a Limousin, and men of that name were tough fellows.

There had been a soft, thick fall of snow the day before; the cold of the night and the utter stillness left every branch piled deep with it, except some more supple ones that had bent under the white weight. As we walked along through the woods, the branches stirred, here and there, bending, until there was the sound of fine, powdered snow, striking the earth like the great wing of a moth.

Yet the sun was bright. Its brilliance, I think, made the chill of the air seem yet more biting. By this cold I do not mean that winter frost that most people know, but the true rigor of the North when a hand grows numb almost with the very act of stripping off a glove. There seems to be a dreadful, invisible enemy near, and people are continually looking into the faces of one another to see if the white patch is appearing on cheek or nose.

I stopped to admire a pool in the midst of a clearing. It was quite deep, but it was frozen to the bottom, so that it was a solid bowl of glass. I could count the pebbles on the bottom; I could trace every vein in the leaves of the water plants. My nurse — her face is a blank to me, so that I can see her now with a white mist in place of features — had gone off to see if she had not noted a squirrel aloft in some tree, daring out in the face of such weather to look at the sun and let the sun look at him. I found myself alone by that crystal pool in a tall avenue of hemlocks, when I felt something behind me. I was afraid to turn around.

It was an unseen thing as evil, let me say, as the picture of the old hag in the fairy tale — a nameless dread. I was sure that there were eyes bearing upon me, and, although I could not hear a sound, I sensed that the eyes were drawing closer to me. In a sudden frenzy I whirled around and screamed.

My inner picture had been true. It was a man, not a woman. He had the ugliest face that the sun ever looked upon. Many a time since I have studied that face, and I have never had occasion to change my first judgment. A long, lean face, purple with cold, topped a long, lean body, poorly clothed for that month in the year. He tried to smile at me — reassuringly, I suppose — and I thought that the lips would twist and break with the effort. It was like the grimace of an ogre.

At that I shrieked again and ran as fast as I could, straight past him. Once I felt he was following, and I screamed again until I saw my nurse hurrying toward me — nearly frightened to death, I have no doubt.

What followed, or what she said to that

strange young man, I cannot recall. The rest of that day is lost in a haze, which is strange. One would think that what followed such a shock would be remembered, and not what went before.

However, my adventure of the forest remained in my mind, and the results of it dropped out of my thoughts until the following spring came. Memory then began quite vigorously. From that moment I can keep a straight narrative of the events in my life. It was the time of the first flowers. There was still snow beneath the trees, sometimes heaped up to a prodigious height around the trunks, and covered by a gray crust as strong, almost, as wood. In the shadow of the forest, too, there was still the ghost of winter freezing, but in the open the meadows were beginning to stir with life. The trees were still wretched-looking, starved, black things, some with their bodies split open by the frosts of the cold season; underfoot spring already was smiling.

You dwellers in southern climates have no knowledge of what that first flushing of the spring means to the snowbound peoples of the North — how the blood leaps, and the heart sings at the sight of it. The air is filled with magic; everyone is happy;

there is nothing but smiling; there is never a harsh word.

The season had so worked upon my father — I can attribute it to nothing else — that he declared he would, in person, overlook my first riding lesson. It was the first time in my existence that he had favored me with ten consecutive words, and this made the day one of the great ones of my life. Riding clothes had been made to fit my small self. A pony, guaranteed for perfect temper and gentle gaits, had been bought, and we sallied out for the stables. What I first saw was a glistening, black charger that danced upon the air and tossed his head, his mane flaring up above him until he looked like a giant. I was afraid that I was to be put on the back of this winged monster, but my father laughed and pointed out my horse, a dainty-limbed little creature with an eye every bit as mild and almost as intelligent as the eye of a woman.

The head groom put me up with a toss and a laugh. As he was fitting my feet into the stirrups, I had my first sight of him who held the pony's head. It was the hideous face of my man of the forest. With a wild screech I lost my balance and tumbled backward out of the little saddle.

The head groom caught me and set me on my feet, when I bolted for the house as fast as I could run. Thunder roared behind me. A shining, black thing flashed above me, and then I was snatched up into the heart of the sky — to find myself sitting on the pommel in front of my father. He was in a fury.

"Are you a Limousin? Are you my son? Are you a fool and a little coward?" he said to me through his tight lips. "How do you dare scream like this when the pony has not stirred? Yes, even if it dashed your body to pieces, do you dare to cry out like a girl?"

"It is the forest man!" I cried, sobbing to him. "It is the forest man!" I pointed to the ugly face of the new groom.

What with the shock of that unexpected vision and the overwhelming rage of my father, I passed into a semi-hysteria and could only wail out, again and again: "It is the forest man!" My father grew more and more beside himself with rage. Finally he went back with me slung contemptuously over the crook of his arm, to ask the head groom: "Who is this man?"

"It is Pierre Reynal," said the groom.

"Has he been with you long?"

"For three months, sir."

"His character?"

The head groom looked about him rather wildly for a moment, then found his superlative. "I have given the keeping of *monsieur*'s own horses into his hands!"

It was enough. My father looked on Pierre Reynal, who stood with his cap in his hand, in a very kindly manner.

"You have changed the manners of this black devil, Pierre," he said.

"We get on very well together, he and I," said Pierre Reynal.

He smiled, and I shuddered, remembering that smile and seeing it again. He was the only man I ever knew who was made actually more hideous by a smile.

"What is wrong with my son?" asked my father.

"Ah, sir, would that I knew!"

With this, my father carried me back to the house, strode in, and literally cast me down at the feet of my terrified mother.

"You have given me a son like yourself!" he cried. "He is a fool and a coward . . . a fool and a coward . . . like you, Julie!"

By this time I was screaming again, and my father, with a tortured cry, rushed out of the room, his hands clapped over his ears to keep out the sound.

# Chapter Two

# The New Secretary

You will wonder how a servant could have been on the place for three long months unknown to any of us, but the château, as most people called it, was so large that what happened in one nook of it might very well escape the knowledge of the master of the place. It was his habit to put an absolute authority into the hands of the chiefs of his staff, while he demanded from them, in return, an absolute accounting of all that happened in each department. The chief woodman, for instance, could thin the forest according to his own discretion, but woe to him, if he selected the wrong tree, or one that was essential to the beauty of the estate. The stable master, in the same manner, could hire and discharge, raise wages, buy hay and oats, and do as he chose, but the frightful anxiety which he bore in keeping the horses fit for the inspection of *Monsieur*

Limousin turned his hair white ten years before his time. This was a rule with my father.

"All truly great generals," he was fond of saying, "knew the man to trust and trusted him. The glorious Bonaparte surrounded himself with men who were like hands to him, and brains."

The great Napoléon was my father's god. He began his mature life with a handsome estate, and the nucleus of the château already built near that river that men were beginning to call the Limousin in compliment to my family. From a modest stretch of land it had grown into a small province. In making that property expand, *Monsieur* Limousin had used truly Napoléonic methods. If he wanted to buy the lands of a neighbor, he ruined the man first, by attacking his interests in other directions. He emptied the pockets of his victim by some subtle, swift stock raid in the open market, and, when the poor fellow was destroyed, my father bought the estate for a song. He was hated at first, but afterward he was admired. The difference between sharp practice and good business often lies only in the size of the transaction.

Like the hero he admired, he was magnificent in all his ways. Because the road to the château wound through a wretched little village two miles from the house, he tore that town to the ground and rebuilt it substantially with hewed stone. An excellent architect designed the quaint, old-world houses; an excellent landscape artist designed the park with which he beautified the village still further. When all was ended, the villagers found that they were living in heaven, and that the expense of the change had been borne by a man who asked for no return.

Generosity on such a scale was divine. My father went further.

"It is necessary," I have heard him say many times, "that a strong man be either hated or worshiped."

He chose the second part. He established a bank in the town. Through a capable officer of the bank, he extended loans here and there to the most provident citizens, until in the course of a very little time the lives of the entire body of people lay in his hands. With a gesture he could exalt the lowest to the side of the highest; with a nod he could tumble the loftiest man in the village into the dust.

"How frightfully it must cost you!" cried my simple mother to him one day.

"Silly child," he said. "They are my subjects . . . I am the king, and the interest they pay to me is the taxation I levy on them."

The whole venture, as a matter of fact, he turned from a striking bit of philanthropy into the soundest of good business. The villagers could never see the truth behind the golden mist of his generosity. If, here and there, one of their townsfolk disappeared from their midst and removed to a distant part of the land, it was never suspected that the strong and secret hand of *Monsieur* Limousin was weeding out the indigent and putting in their places diligent workers who would pay fatter rates of interest to his bank. In a very short time, the countryside worshiped him, as he had declared they must. His tenant farmers and his hired laborers were the chosen stock of the countryside, and the whole district looked toward the lofty walls of the château, bulking above the ancient trees, as toward a heavenly place from which peace and good will flowed forth over the world.

It is said that no man is a hero to his valet, but I doubt if a single one of *Monsieur* Limousin's domestics ever looked behind the veil into his inner self. Far be it even for me to pretend to pierce to the complete truth concerning him. I put down only what my eyes saw, and my ears heard, in the hope that you may be helped to build the picture of a man whose vices and virtues were like himself — great and strong.

My half-brother, Hubert Guillaume Limousin, was like Father, tall, rugged, powerful even in his sixteenth year. He had a handsome, dark face like the portrait of *Monsieur* Limousin's first wife that hung in the library opposite my father's chair, above the fireplace. I have heard that even her fiery heart was broken by the imprisoning strength of *Monsieur* Limousin's will. However he may have regarded her during her life, it is certain that after her death he loved her, and loved the image of her in her son. Hubert was the only person in Canada, I am sure, who dared to stand face to face with my father; he was the only person who could pretend to read his mind, because they were so much alike in furious temper, in physical strength, and in wits that were always at work even in the very midst of the most headlong, uncontrollable temper.

To Hubert my mother went on this day of days, to ask him why my father was in such a fury. He had his hat in one hand and a supple, riding whip in the other. As he looked down on me from the height of his years and his strength, I feared and worshiped him as my mother feared and worshiped her husband.

"I'm sure I cannot tell," said Hubert, "unless it's because Jean is such a frightful little sniveler. Look at him now!"

After Hubert left the room, my mother drew the whole story out of me by patient degrees, and at last she went with me to see the new groom for herself. We did not go near the stable, for while we were still at a distance she stopped with a little shiver and cried softly to me: "That is the man, Jean?"

"It is he!" I said. Pierre Reynal was about to ride a horse to its exercise.

"Ah, then I understand," she whispered. She hurried me back to the house, murmuring: "Why could not François understand, also?"

There was an instant sympathy between my mother and me, of flesh to flesh and soul to soul. She had given me her own frail body, her golden hair, her blue eyes, her delicate, pretty face which I so often groaned against as I stood before the mirror yearning with a broken heart for the stalwart shoulders and the dark, stern features of a true Limousin. With the body, she gave me the same spirit, also. Shall I tell you that I knew the shadow in her mind while she was still smiling, or that, before I awakened at night from an evil dream, she was already beside my bed?

She waited until the next day so that the temper of my father might soften a little. Much as she dreaded him, she could not help raising her voice on my behalf. The next morning she said to him: "I went to see Pierre Reynal, and I could not help shuddering at his frightful face. François, you must forgive poor little Jean."

At this he knit his fingers in his beard and stared at her after a fashion of his.

"Pierre Reynal is a flawless horseman," was all he said. Then he added, still watching her: "I find that he is a fellow of education, too. I am considering promoting him to a better place in the household!"

And he did. Now, as I consider it, I try to tell myself that he could not have done the thing merely to torture his wife and his youngest son. I try to tell myself that he had found an opportunity to look into the mind of this new groom at the stables, that he had seen something extraordinary in the skill with which the man had mastered those fiery devils, the Thoroughbreds of the Limousin stock. I tell myself that he had seen or guessed at other qualities in Reynal that were worthy of confidence. The education alone of Reynal, considering his place in the world, was a thing to be wondered at.

However, I must end explanations and come to the thing itself. A few days later the secretary who kept the correspondence and prepared the letters of *Monsieur* Limousin was discharged. Still another week went by. Then, one evening, as I came into the library to say good night to my mother and father — Hubert was then away at school — *Monsieur* touched a bell.

Presently there advanced into the room a tall man, dressed in black, with his throat muffled in a sort of old-fashioned black stock. He came slowly into the light, so that I saw all of these funereal details before I saw the face itself, and then I grew giddy and weak, and my mother caught me quickly to her. There in the clothes of a gentleman was my wild man of the forest, the late groom of the stables, the pale, hideous face of Pierre Reynal.

There was just an instant of pause and silence during which I could hear the heavy breathing of my father as though he drank in the picture with a savage satisfaction. Then his voice lifted me to my feet.

"Stand up to meet the gentleman, Jean. And, my dear, I wish you to know my new secretary, who is to be one of us and will try to keep my very tangled affairs in a better order. This is Pierre Reynal."

I can remember, as distinctly as I recall the terror with which I went forward to give my hand to the stranger, that the forehead of the monster was glistening with perspiration. By that I judged, afterward, that the moment had been as grim a trial to him as it had been to us.

However, from that moment Pierre Reynal was a regular member of the family.

# Chapter Three

# The Werewolf

If it be true that my father brought Pierre Reynal into the house only for the sake of plaguing my poor mother and myself, it is equally true that, at the end of a few days, he was convinced that Pierre Reynal was a treasure in his new post. My father found the greatest pleasure in pointing out to us the excellent qualities of his new secretary. He would say: "Consider his soft step, his grave manner. Are they not the qualities of a gentleman?"

At this I remember my mother broke out into one of her little flurries. "François, François! You know that he has the step of a cat and the manner of an owl. I am afraid of him . . . my very bones quake at the sight of him."

To this her husband answered, with a smile that showed his youthful, white teeth: "You have a charming imagination,

24

my dear. You might have been a poet, if you had been born to wear trousers. However, I say that I see in Pierre Reynal the making of a gentleman. He has the qualities of which I have spoken. In addition, he is never officious, never forward, never boisterous. He remains in the house as quiet as a shadow."

"He is a shadow, indeed," said my mother.

"For the rest, I discover new accomplishments in him every day. In the open, he is a master horseman. Within doors, he is the most efficient accountant, has the most reliable memory, is the most careful and exact secretary that I have ever enjoyed. Why should you not welcome him as a gentleman?"

Although he insisted that Pierre Reynal be received as a gentleman, his own treatment of his secretary was that which one would give to a highly trained dog, say. He was fond of drawing out Reynal in a manner somewhat like this: "You speak an excellent French, Pierre. It has a Parisian quality that is rare in this barbaric Northland. And your English is very good . . . not like the French, but very good. Have you any other languages?"

"A morsel of Italian, sir."

"Italian, also? Italian, also? You are a man of many tongues. A three-tongued man, Pierre Reynal . . . more accomplished than a snake, by half, at least."

My father was very fond of his own jokes, and here he broke into the heartiest laughter, rocking himself back and forth in his big chair until even its sturdy frame groaned with the bulk of him. This laughter always ended in a prolonged chuckling during which he combed his heavy, curling beard with his fingers.

By such bits of dialogue as this I came to know that *Monsieur,* in reality, looked down upon the man just as much as my mother did — without the same horror, of course. I once asked her why he kept Pierre Reynal in the house.

She took my face between her hands. To see her so grave and so sad was like watching a garden under shadow. "God will not let me tell you," she said, "and I pray that you never come to know."

"But Pierre Reynal, why does he stay when he is treated so by my father?"

"Because he is very proud," said my mother.

"Is there pride in the devil, too?" I asked.

After that she would talk no more, but

hurried me off to bed. I lay awake for a time, fearing the dark. When I closed my eyes, the terrible face of Reynal formed in the blackness and grinned at me. At length, tired of terror itself, I fell asleep.

I was wakened by the cold hand of the moon upon my face. The great French door that opened on the balcony was white with it, worked across by the regular shadow of a climbing vine, like graceful stone tracery. Between me and the door was the form of a long, oval head — the head of Pierre Reynal! Yes, he was kneeling by my bed, leaning over me. When I drew my breath, he was up and away. Before the scream began, he was gliding through the door and across the balcony.

When my mother came flying to me and I gasped out the story, she picked me up in her arms with a moan like a tortured dove. Anger gave her strength to carry me lightly into her own room and through it to the chamber of her husband. Apparently the shriek had reached even his ear, for we found him standing in a red dressing robe, combing his black beard.

"My Jean was waked out of his sleep by your pet demon, Reynal, leaning over his bed. Look at his face. Look at his face, François. You are killing him!"

27

At this my father uttered a little exclamation and strode across the room, making chair and table and lamp quiver with the weight of his step.

"Are you armed, François?" cried my mother.

My father was gone, and my mother sat down on the edge of his bed to soothe me. He came back in a moment, smiling with anger.

"Reynal was in his bed, fast asleep," he said. "His door on the balcony is locked, and the key is lost. Now take the brat away and never mention his cowardly dreams to me again!"

My mother carried me back to my bed and stayed with me.

"But you," I whispered to her, "you believe me? It was not a dream?"

"Hush, dear," she said. "Oh, we are lost, we are lost."

That frightened little whisper of hers was like the sigh of a ghost. It filled me with so much dread that I fell asleep under the black weight of it, feeling that Pierre Reynal would never leave the Château Limousin until both my mother and I were dead.

Aside from that strange incursion into

my room that night I cannot say that the actions of Reynal were ever unusual or ominous in any way. He had an odd habit of taking long walks by himself. Usually he left the house just before dusk, and often he did not return until after dinner. When he came in, those were the only occasions on which we ever saw his pale face flushed or his eye lighted.

It was while Reynal was off on one of these woodland rambles through the dark, that I came into the library, according to the rule, to say good night. At the same moment my father leaned his head to the side, then stood up, hastily unlocked and opened the door that led from the library into the garden. A dank breath of night and mist blew into the room and set me shivering. Then, out of the far horizon of blackness, we heard the cry of a timber wolf.

"Julie," said *Monsieur*, "is not this the month of the werewolf?"

I turned a wild eye on my mother and found her with hands clasped and her face white. Of course, the same hideous thought had been born at the same instant in both our minds. *Monsieur* shut the door, and, as he turned to us, he was smiling. Can it be that he knew how his casual words would sink into our very souls? I cannot believe it. For all these years I have not dared believe it.

You must not think that these things happened in quick succession, as they appear in this writing. They were scattered through much time. Only, looking back on those days from this distance, I give the peaks and summits of our quiet life, and omit many long valleys that lie between the hills.

I think that I had come, now, to my ninth year, and my mother decided that something must be done to take me from the château, for I had begun to fear my own shadow. I could not sleep without a light in the room; I dared not walk in the woods alone; I would not even paddle a canoe close to the dark margin of the lake where the trees overhung it.

She went to her husband, and declared I had now reached an age when, because of my reading and thinking beyond my years, she no longer could teach me as I should be taught. I should be sent away to a school, as my brother, Hubert Guillaume, had been sent before me. *Monsieur* laughed the thought away. He took hold of my upper arm; his thumbs and forefinger overlapped around it.

"Send him away?" he said. "Nonsense, Julie! Look at him, my dear, and then suggest it again. He is as light as a puff of smoke. The first cold wind of public opinion would dissolve him. The first schoolboy prank would drive him into hysteria and a madhouse. Send him away? No, he must be kept at home where you will continue to coddle him and keep his soul and his body united. As for the teaching, we will bring home a tutor to attend to that."

When he spoke in such a tone, she never could answer him, but it was like a death-blow to both of us. We wept together under the stroke that had fallen, but neither of us thought of appeal, far less of revolt. So it was that the tutor came into the house.

He was selected because of two qualifications. For the rest, he was a man of past forty, with a withered, handsome face and the habitual sneer of a clever man who has failed in the world. As for his qualifications, my father announced them to Argen in their first interview, in his usual loud voice — so that I heard every word as I sat in the next room. *Monsieur* was a man who believed in saying what he had to say so that everyone could hear him. He had not the slightest care whether or not his sentiments would be approved of by his servants — or his wife and sons.

To Bertram Argen he said: "You are here, *Monsieur* Argen, because of two qualities which you possess. The first and less important reason is that you are a man of education, familiar with the ways of the world, and capable of polite manners and conversation. The second and more important reason is that you come of an ancient name and your blood is blue. It is on account of the second reason that I am paying you a salary that is probably twice your actual worth. You will understand, *Monsieur* Argen, that you are about to undertake the instruction of a son of the house of Limousin, and that the blood of the Bourbons flows in the veins of that boy. There is another point that you must comprehend from the beginning. In this house there is only one master, and the rest of the household serves his will. Needless to say, sir, I am that master."

A few moments afterward, Argen came in to me. I knew by his icy smile that he had submitted to the tyrant, but that he would make me suffer for his submission.

# Chapter Four

# The Feat

There was a pair of excellent reasons for the hatred that Argen felt for me. On the one hand, the sternness of *Monsieur* filled my tutor with malice; on the other hand, I was one of those unattractive boys who melt into tears at the least provocation. That is a weakness that is irritating in girls. It is both bewildering and disgusting in boys.

Mathematics is as mysterious as a ghost language to me, and my very first lesson in that science brought a tirade from Argen that sent me with my tears and my troubles to my mother. She came with me to the schoolroom and spoke calmly but severely to the tutor. Argen astonished both of us by announcing that my teaching was entirely in his hands, and that he was not to receive advice from more than one person in the house — meaning, of course, *Monsieur.*

It was true. My father gave me entirely into the hands of this waspish fellow, and, during four hours every day, he turned my life into a torment. However, I got on, for next to the face of Pierre Reynal and the frown of my father, I dreaded the biting tongue of my tutor. I learned that the only way to avoid its stings was to present perfect lessons. You will guess that the greatest praise I received from him was silence. Yet we covered such ground that at the end of a month Argen could show my work to my father with satisfaction.

This gave my father one of those openings of which he never failed to take advantage.

"You see," he said to my mother, "that even you have not been able to ruin entirely the temper of the boy. There is still metal in him that responds to hammering."

He exchanged a smile with Argen, while my poor mother hung her head and turned white.

Argen, in fact, grew daily in importance and began to push Pierre Reynal into the background. If Reynal interested my father because of the peculiar influence that he exercised over my mother and me, Argen was still more worthwhile because he directly entertained *Monsieur* and afforded him company. We never entertained people of our own station.

I suppose my father had not a friend in the world that he could treat on an equal footing. He was surrounded entirely by the peasants and the villagers to whom he was a god, by the household in which he was a king among slaves, and, at a greater distance, by the hatred and the bitterness of all the world with which he came into contact through his business affairs. Argen was, therefore, the first man to sit at his table in years, who was capable of telling a story that was worth hearing or narrating personal experiences worthy of a place in a book of adventure. Better than all this, he was a perfect listener. His attitude toward my father was that of an equal; he was at ease to make himself into an audience. At the same time there was an exquisite consciousness on both sides that he was no more than a superior domestic.

In this manner, Argen was rising more and more in power. Two fine horses were assigned to him for his use; his room was changed to one of the most pleasant chambers on the south side of the château, overlooking the river. Here my father occasionally condescended to go for a bottle of wine in the evening, and for talk that was not meant for the ears of my mother.

It was at this point that Pierre Reynal, by an odd stroke that seemed nothing at the time, completely overturned the domestic hierarchy, and again put himself at the top of the heap.

It was a fall day. The trees were naked, but the air was not yet bitterly cold. A pleasant blue mist veiled the woodland. A new rifle had come for my father, and he was out early after breakfast to try it. He was so excited over it that everyone was invited to come out with him. We stood around in a well-ordered semicircle and watched. His skill was extraordinary, for he was not only a great hunter, but he practiced constantly at a target. We saw him take aim and first shoot a bottle from the top of a post, then shatter a little pebble on the same post. At that distance, the stone was hardly more than a twinkling point of light as the morning sun struck on it.

We applauded regularly, of course, like a perfectly disciplined household. My father was in ecstasies over his weapon. He handed it to Argen and bade him note this and that perfection in the rifle, but Argen showed by his very manner of holding the weapon that he knew nothing about it.

"When you are in the wilderness, you

must be a barbarian, Argen!" cried my father. "This is not the Old World. Do you see that twisted old oak? Under that very tree, my friend, the Hurons murdered one of my forefathers, his wife, and his three daughters . . . and ripped away their scalps. Was it not under that very tree, Julie? If you are to stay with us, you must learn by that example, Argen. In this Canada of ours, and in the Château Limousin, one is either the scalper or the scalped."

Here he broke off with a hearty laughter at his jest, and walked back and forth, combing his black beard with his fingers and shrugging his shoulders. He was like an actor on a stage, except that this actor knew the audience dared not hiss. Next he began to wish for some more difficult target to test fully the merits of this straight-shooting rifle.

Now Pierre Reynal made his suggestion. "I have heard," he said, "of a pigeon tied by a leg and allowed to fly."

He had no sooner made that suggestion than my father took it up with enthusiasm. He caused a pigeon to be brought and fastened by one leg with a long cord. The poor thing at once took the air and flew straight up, was stopped by the jerk of the string that tumbled it half the way to the ground again, regained its balance by a miracle of grace, and slid away to the side until the cord stopped it again. In the midst of these lively maneuvers my father took his aim with great care and fired. Although one or two feathers fluttered to the ground, the bird did not fall.

"I shall nail it this time!" My father tipped the rifle up to his shoulders again.

"Hold, *Monsieur* Limousin!" said Pierre Reynal.

My father stared at him as though he had heard the voice of a madman, for I suppose the word called him back to the days of his childhood. Not since that period, I have no doubt, had he heard a man say stop to him. Pierre Reynal had stepped out a little from the semicircle of spectators.

"You must not shoot again at that bird, *Monsieur,*" he said with the same surprising air of authority.

"I must not? *I* must not?" cried my father, growing a little flushed.

"It is the rule," said Reynal. "You have missed, and the pigeon cannot lose its life. It has earned its freedom."

*Monsieur* hesitated, as though he balanced between a desire to slaughter and a desire to obey the rules of the game as Reynal had suggested. "Well," he said at last, "carry the pigeon back to the cote."

"Even that will not do," Pierre Reynal explained. "It must be set free. Cut the string, man, and toss the pigeon into the air."

On the estate of Limousin, men did not wait to be bidden twice. When an order was heard, it was obeyed. Therefore, the pigeon-keeper did not pause to hear a confirmation from *Monsieur* Limousin. He seemed to take it for granted that, if Pierre Reynal dared to speak at all, he must have authority behind him. Therefore, he cut the string, and the pigeon shot away over the barren tops of the trees and was lost in the autumn mist. I hardly saw it go, even though my heart leaped with joy because of its escape; I was too busy studying my father's face. I recognized that savage flush of deep, deep red that settled upon his face, and a great exultation poured through my body.

"See," I said to my mother — for I was standing at her side. "See, now. He will tear Pierre Reynal limb from limb."

Who could read the mind of my father? He lived by opposites. The little affront that seemed so great, offered as it was to so perfect a tyrant, this stroke at the face of the lion, which made him spread his claws, in another moment appeared to please him as much as it had angered him. He clapped his hand against the stock of the rifle and began to laugh.

"You are a stern taskmaster, Reynal," he said. "You are very harsh to me, Reynal. But now, by heaven, *you* shall shoot at the next bird. If I were you, Reynal, I should try very hard to hit the mark!"

There was a very apparent threat in the last remark, but Reynal was so busy looking over the rifle that *Monsieur* had handed to him, that he did not seem to notice the inflection of my father's voice. While the second pigeon was brought out and fixed to the end of the long string, Reynal was preparing the weapon.

"I shall not miss, however," Reynal said, still looking at the rifle rather than the target. "Besides, this is a pleasant rifle and will shoot straight."

"You will not be able to put any blame upon the rifle, Reynal," said my father dryly. "Now let us see you shoot!"

The others thought it very wonderful. For my part, I had not the slightest doubt as to what would happen. When the tall man with the hideous face picked up the rifle, it seemed to me that the pigeon was already fluttering on the ground. Neither had mother any doubt. She was turning away before the rifle spoke. I looked back and saw the bird whirl in the air and then tumble to the ground. We could even hear the soft thump as it struck.

From what I knew of my father, I expected him to be thrown into a jealous transport by this feat. Again I read him wrong. He clapped Pierre Reynal upon the shoulder and broke into congratulations.

"Most wonderful of all," he cried, "you have not had a weapon in your hands for how many years?"

"You are wrong, *Monsieur*. I use a gun every day."

"What? Am I deaf, then?"

"*Monsieur* must understand that to practice with a weapon, one must not necessarily discharge it."

Never had I seen my father so surprised or so impressed. He even gave back a pace from Reynal and regarded him anew from head to foot.

"I have misjudged you, my friend," he said at last. "But now I understand you, I shall make up for these neglected years."

# Chapter Five

# Reynal

My father loved the sports of the field passionately, and he cared for men almost in proportion as they excelled in those sports. His one greatest regret, I think, was that he had no companion for his hunting trips. Now he had found one in Reynal. Before the sun set on that same day, the two were away for the forest and did not appear again at the house for a full forty-eight hours. When they came, my father wore a serious face. His leather hunting coat was torn to ribbons on one side, and there was a shallow cut across his forehead, and, also, he went with a limp. He never referred to the thing that had happened. Neither did Pierre Reynal whisper a word of it to a living human being. Within the week a mysterious knowledge was spread over the estate. Everyone knew, or thought they knew, that my father had failed to bring down a charging moose, that he had been struck down by the monster and almost killed, when a perfect shot from the rifle of Reynal killed the giant on the spot.

Why my father should have failed to mention the thing, I cannot tell. It was not vanity; his vanity did not take that form. He was always fairly willing to expose his weaknesses and his failures in the belief that, when known, they merely served to accent the greatness of his real strength. I think that he remained quiet in the expectation that Reynal would, someday, speak of the affair. Reynal never did, and upon that bit of reticence rather than upon the actual saving of his life, I believe that my father based the great regard that he had for Reynal from that moment thence forward. Although Reynal had simply been a groom in the beginning, growing into importance as a means of tormenting my mother and me, he had finally stepped inside the very mind of my father, becoming — I speak without exaggeration — the greatest friend of a friendless man.

We felt the effects in the house the very next night in a strange scene. It was my tenth birthday, and in honor of the occasion I supped with the family and afterward sat with them to hear Argen sing. One of the airs was a lively waltz, and Father began to clap his hands in rhythm to it.

"There is a dance!" he cried. "There is something to tickle your feet, Julie, my dear. If I were a dancing man . . . but . . . here is a man who will do as well or better. Reynal, will you ask *Madame* Limousin to dance? Argen, play that thing again . . . with feeling, man . . . with feeling!"

He was laughing again, and his black eyes flashed with a terrible fire as he saw Reynal drawn from his chair, while my mother stood up.

"I may have this honor?" Reynal said, moving across the room and bowing before my mother.

"You may, sir," she said in a dying voice, and straightway glided away with him in the dance.

If she was almost fainting, instinct and the fear of François kept her feet sliding in perfect rhythm. This strange Reynal waltzed beautifully; it was like seeing an angel's grace in the form of a demon. And never did the monster seem more like a devil to me than he did when he held my lovely mother in his arms, and circled around the room like a black eagle swooping toward the aerie with the white dove in its talons! What went on in the mind of

Reynal, no one ever could guess, because a round, white scar in the center of his right cheek had puckered all the flesh on that side of his face, drawing his mouth into its habitual, frightful grin — which a real smile made more devilish than ever.

When they had finished dancing to the tune once, my father insisted that they dance again. He seemed to be enjoying it as much as a connoisseur at the opera, leaning far back in his chair and waving one hand in time — a graceful hand that marked every change and undulation of the music by a difference in its gesture.

As soon as the dance ended, however, my mother had to leave the room. I went with her as a matter of course. The door was hardly closed behind her when she told me to support her. I led her to a window and opened it. The cold air revived her, and then I supported her upstairs.

On the way she kept repeating: "Did you hear, Jean? Did you hear, my poor boy?"

As we left the room, my father had been saying to Reynal: "My most all-accomplished Pierre, is there anything among the graces of the world beyond the tips of your fingers? Is there nothing that lies beyond you? Then tell me, Pierre

Reynal . . . will you take this girl-faced son of mine and guarantee to make a man of him? Argen shall teach his brain to be clever . . . you will teach his soul to become the strong soul of a man. Could you do that, Pierre Reynal?"

The answer of Reynal was bold as a bugle blast. "Sir, I shall transform him within a year."

My mother wept over me, crying: "It is done, Jean. He has taken you from me at last."

In the middle of the next afternoon, my father sent for me. I found him in his business room, against the ancient darkness of the paneled walls of that lofty apartment, his florid face, black beard, and shining eyes looked like a 17th-century painting. By the window, tall and lithe as an Indian, his arms folded across his breast, was Pierre Reynal.

"From this day," said my father in a solemn voice, "you are more the pupil of Reynal than of Argen." He made a pause, then went on: "When he speaks to you, consider that it is my voice."

He could not have said more to make me understand that Reynal had me completely in his hands. Five minutes later Reynal and

I were in the woods, he walking with his gliding step, and I stuttering and stumbling over rocks and roots, for fear is an intoxication of the blood.

When we came to the bank of the river, he said: "Take off your clothes and walk in."

"I cannot swim," I said.

He made no answer, and, when I looked up to his face with its strange sneer, I was sure that he intended a simple end for me — death by drowning that would be imputed to accident. However, I could not resist. I took off my clothes, and, standing trembling in the chilly air on the bank, I took a last look upon the world. It did not seem so beautiful a place that one should weep at the leaving of it. A thought of my mother came in my mind, but before it should completely unnerve me, I stepped in the icy waters of the river. I walked till the water was up to my knees, to my hips, to my chest. As I paused there with the cold driving all the breath from my lungs, I heard the harsh voice of Reynal saying: "It is enough. Come back."

Go back to him? No, the black river was far better — far better to feel one moment of choking and pain and then drift down the current with the other bits of branches and boughs that flecked its surface. I cast myself boldly forward, floundered for a moment with feet and hands, and then sank.

Such things are not forgotten. I can remember at this instant with perfect vividness the shadowy swirl of the currents beneath me, and the dark, sliding arm of a branch that floated past above my head. It was not an agony. There was a struggling, choking moment. I felt myself dying when a power caught me and jerked me up to light and air again.

By the time my senses had ceased whirling, Pierre Reynal had carried me back to the shore. With the edge of his hand he whipped the water from my body. Then he wrung the water from my hair, which my mother kept long. After that, he bade me dress, and I obeyed. I remember that my chief wonder was that he asked no questions, and that he could stand so quietly at ease in his soaked clothes with the sharp wind blowing against him.

When I was dressed, he waved me before him. "Run!" he said.

I ran with all my might, feeling that the devil was behind me. When I was blind and sick with exhaustion, I stopped and leaned against a tree.

Pierre Reynal stood before me, hardly breathing. "Is that all?" he asked.

"That is all I can do," I answered.

"Ah, well," murmured Pierre Reynal, "there is much to be done, truly."

He took me back to the house. On the edge of the woods he paused again.

"Tell me, *Monsieur* Jean," he said.

"Yes, *Monsieur* Reynal?" I responded, still panting.

"Why do you hate me so?"

I felt that if I made such an admission, I should be lost entirely beyond hope. "No, no!" I insisted. "I do not hate you, sir. I have a great fondness for you, *Monsieur* Reynal."

"Can you look at me and say that?"

I looked up into his face. "Sir," I began, "I have a . . . a great. . . ."

He began to smile that terrible death's head smile of his, and I could not utter another syllable.

"Let us go on," he said, and we went on into the house.

This was the beginning of my lessons at the hand of Pierre Reynal. He taught me to swim, to dive without making a great splashing, to run smoothly and effortlessly; he taught me how to walk softly; how to ride a horse and talk to it; how to load a gun and shoot it; he taught me the names of birds, beasts, insects, grasses, and flowers. He carried me into the very heart of nature.

Doing these things, you will say: "How could any mortal fail to learn to love such a teacher?"

I, being concerned with the truth, only, and not with possibilities, must confess that at the end of it all, I felt nothing but a greater aversion for Pierre Reynal than I had felt when he was only an unknown to me. The more I knew of him, the more mysteriously distasteful did he become.

But here I must make a pause to speak of my half-brother and of how he came home.

# Chapter Six

# The Return of Hubert

The return of my half-brother grew greater and greater in importance with each year; each year brought closer the moment when he would leave his college and return to the château to live his life. That is to say, this was the plan for which my father hoped and prayed.

It was true that the only creature whom my father loved in this world was the one creature who dared to lift head and defy him. Sometimes I have thought that it was owing to the very love he bore the boy that Hubert dared to be so bold before his terrible father. He knew that wild affection, and therefore he imposed upon his father. I have told myself that to explain what would seem, otherwise, a most unnatural boldness and courage on the part of a youngster before such a man as my father.

Yet it is not true. I can see the events of those old years in a clearer light of reason and understanding now. Among other things, I am sure that Hubert Guillaume Limousin defied Father simply out of the largeness of a spirit similar to his. Each was a mirror for the other. The soul of François Limousin was the soul of Hubert Limousin.

When I think of myself, viewing the things that followed, I think of a mouse looking forth from its hole upon the battle of two tigers. There was always some subject for combat between them, but the principal matter of debate was always the future of Hubert. He was by no means wedded to the thought of a life spent at the château, and when he burst into one of his rages — which were every week of his vacation times at home — he was sure to declare his intention of becoming a lawyer.

On this occasion, Hubert came home a man. He had been a boy at Christmas, but he returned a man. At Christmas he had been nineteen; now he was twenty. I felt as though ten years had passed over him. When I first saw him, I shrank from him, as usual, because he had a peculiar talent for making me miserable. On this day he paused a moment over me and took hold on me, laying his broad thumbs in the hollows of my shoulders.

"Why," said Hubert, "our little Jean is out of dresses at last, I think."

You observe that, even when Hubert had softened, his tongue was still sharp. I was so astonished at winning even this much attention from him that I trembled with delight. He turned to Pierre Reynal.

"I have heard that you are working with him. Well, this is very fine . . . this is very fine! There is color in his cheeks, and his eyes are brighter and . . . *phew!* What an arm he is getting!"

"Hubert," I broke out, "I can swim four hundred yards! I swear that it is true!"

At this he laughed, and his voice had so deepened that there was a thunderous undertone that reminded me weirdly of the laughter of my father.

When Limousin himself saw Hubert, before they had touched hands, he cried out: "By heavens, Hubert, you are my height to a hair breadth!"

"But I lack a good many hair breadths of having your shoulders," said Hubert.

"That will come when you are a man, my boy," said *Monsieur.*

"Do you think," Hubert probed, "that I am so far from being a man now?" That was the first note of war.

We all sat at the lunch table together.

"And what have you been doing lately?" said Limousin. "Besides the crew work, what have you been doing of interest?"

Hubert threw up his fine head, which was his way before making a dangerous statement. He was like father in this, also: he was always free to tell the world his business and his thoughts. If the world approved, very well, if the world did not approve, it could go to the devil.

"I have been playing cards a good deal," said Hubert. "Next to the crew, that was the most important thing. Yes, even more important."

He knew that he was treading heavily on the toes of Father. Gambling was a vice that Limousin did not have, and, therefore, he hated it.

"You have not, however, been playing for money," said my father, with that dangerous smile of his in which his even white teeth showed behind the beard.

"I have, however, been playing for money. Everyone does."

"You know my mind on that subject, Hubert?"

"One cannot be a booby, sir, when all of

one's companions are doing a thing. . . ."

There would have been an explosion instantly, but it was the first day of Hubert's vacation, and, therefore, *Monsieur* withheld his hand. He merely developed the subject, keeping his voice under control, although my mother and I, feeling so much danger near, stopped eating and watched for the crisis.

"I suppose," said my father, "that you were led on because you have had beginner's luck?"

"Not at all," Hubert answered. "I lost from the first, and kept on playing for fear they should think that I minded the loss."

"So!" said *Monsieur.*

He did not mind spending great sums of money even for small ends, but he hated to throw money away. I do not think, for instance, that he ever gave a penny to charity unless he counted on getting a return for his seeming generosity. Now he was very angry, but he raised his wine glass.

"I drink to your better fortune, Hubert," he said.

"You are very kind, sir."

They drank to one another. The rest of us tasted the wine timidly, hoping that the cloud had blown over. But, alas, it was only beginning.

It was Hubert, driven on by a fierce imp of the perverse, who pursued the question now.

"However," he explained, "my losses are not very high. Eleven hundred dollars would cover the total . . . but they are very pressing. Of course, my friends expect their checks by the first mail after my arrival home."

Hubert felt little assurance on this point, therefore he expressed much. It was his way. It was the way of *Monsieur.*

"They expect your checks by the first mail?" *Monsieur* repeated, smiling wickedly. "Ah, yes."

Why could not Hubert leave well enough alone? There was nothing up to the last penny of *Monsieur*'s fortune that Hubert could not have wheedled from him, but he disdained wheedling. Again he was *Monsieur.*

So he said calmly: "They will not be disappointed, I presume, sir."

"They will not be disappointed?" echoed my father, with the terrible thunder beginning to rumble in his voice. "I cannot tell. I cannot tell. It is a matter, Hubert, which depends upon your conduct . . . your good conduct."

The smile of Hubert was the smile of

*Monsieur;* there was a small white spot in the pit of either cheek.

"My conduct, sir," he said, "I shall attempt to make all that you desire."

"Good! Then we have heard the last concerning this foolish stuff . . . this law?"

I, who sat next to Hubert, heard the gritting of his teeth.

"I trust," he said aloud, "that I do not understand you, sir."

"And why do you trust that?"

"Because for the moment," Hubert responded, "it seems that you are bargaining with me, sir."

"I am a business man, Hubert, and I offer you a business proposition. Give up your ambition for the law . . . consent to settle down at the château. Give me your word for it, and I pay these debts."

*"Monsieur,"* Hubert said, sitting stiff and straight, "these gambling debts are matters of honor. I should be a ruined man, sir, if they were not paid instantly!"

"Beyond a doubt. Beyond a doubt. I am considering all that. Therefore, I make you a proposition that you have such a great reason for closing with instantly."

Hubert quickly stood up from his chair. *"Monsieur,"* he said in a voice that was no more than a whisper, although it almost made me faint in my chair, "*Monsieur,* I am your son."

"You are my son," said my father. "Sit down, Hubert!"

"You are attempting, sir, to strike a bargain on the honor of your son."

*Monsieur* bounded up, and all the china and glass on the table gave out a musical, shivering sound. He struck his hands together. "Do you hear me, young fool? A little more such talk as this, and I send you from the room! My word has been passed! And now I shall confirm it with my oath, Hubert. If I do not have your instant promise to do in all things as I bid you . . . and if I do not have your apology for your present conduct and language, I shall not pay one penny of your gambling debts. Do you hear me?"

*"Monsieur,"* Hubert said, "I cannot listen when my father dishonors himself and me!" He walked from the room.

You are astonished, as I was astonished then, that my father let him go. It was the very intensity of *Monsieur*'s rage at being so bearded that chained him to the place. When he recovered himself, I saw all the rage disappear from his contorted features, and fear take its place. It was a ghostly thing to watch. He was almost like a frightened boy as he ran to the chair of my mother.

"Julie," he whispered — a great moaning whisper — "did he go up to his room? Did you hear his step upon the stairs?"

"Yes," said my trembling mother.

*Monsieur* threw up his great arms. "Help me . . . pity me, God!" he gasped out, and leaped to the door, shouting: "Hubert! Hubert! I retract, Hubert! Hubert, do you hear?"

This was his voice that filled the room with thunder, but as he tore open the door, we heard distinctly the explosion of a revolver in a distant part of the house.

*Monsieur* reeled against the wall with his hands clutched over his face, as though the bullet had gone through his own brain.

# Chapter Seven

# A Saint

All night I slept and wakened, wakened and slept, like a soldier about to be called for a dangerous duty. In the morning we learned that my father had gone to bed at the usual time. At least, he had retired to his room, as though ashamed that even the death of his son could be suspected of breaking in upon his habits and his mental poise. But when the house was dark and quiet, he had stolen out to range up and down the woods.

When we gathered at the breakfast table, my mother and I in black, as a matter of course, we found *Monsieur* dressed in a suit of gay Scotch tweed with a bright little crimson flower in his buttonhole.

"You are late! You are late!" he cried as I came into the room behind my mother. "But that is due to the strange warmth of this weather. I have never seen such a June. Have you, Julie? You must get out into the woods after breakfast. The trees have growing pains . . . they groan, I tell you. And while you stop to light a cigarette . . . a flower turns from a bud to a blossom under your eyes. Oh, it is delightful, Julie!"

One could see by this that he had chosen to act that part which would be least expected of him. The world looked to see him bear himself in the manner of the chief actor in a tragedy. Therefore, he chose to disappoint them and cast the part of a springtime comedy.

He was always acting. Even his bluntness, his frankness on all occasions, was an affectation, too. He was never truly himself, but what he wished himself to be. It required, often, very great acting, but acting it always remained. I do not think that other people saw this, for other people were mature, whereas I was a child. And a sensitive child sees things that the mature eye disregards.

My mother murmured some sort of polite answer. She was as baffled as ever, as remote from understanding *Monsieur*. She would have been frightfully shocked by this light tone if she had not known that he loved the boy who was dead more than he loved all the world that was left alive.

"I am touched," went on *Monsieur,* "to

see that you and *your* boy have put on black for Hubert Guillaume."

These were the very words that he flung at us like a leveled gun. If you say that no man could have been so dastardly, I nevertheless assure you that this is the truth. My mother cringed. A devilish pleasure came into his eyes. He raised the whip again.

"A kind concern for Hubert," went on *Monsieur,* "but, my dear, is it not a little stupid? Just a little stupid?" He leaned and smiled at her.

"I have only meant to do what was right . . . what you would approve of, François," she said.

"Well! But this is a point on which I have never given you instruction, is it not? And, therefore, you cannot expect to know a lesson when you have never had a chance to read the book in which it is written? Well, I must admit all of that. But let me teach you now. May I teach you, my dear wife?"

These were his words, but it is impossible for me to convey the full devilishness of his drawling voice.

"You may do as you please," said my mother, beginning to tremble.

"Well, my dear Julie, I wish to point out that such a concern is cruel, at the bottom.

For do you think that Hubert Guillaume has left this world and been dissipated into nothingness? Do you think that the hundred and seventy-odd pounds of cold flesh lying upstairs is all that remains of Hubert Guillaume?"

My mother gasped and clung to the edge of the table, her eyes half closed. Frightful though it is to tell it, even from this distance of years — he saw her as she was and — struck her again.

"No, François! I do not think that!"

"You forget your breakfast," said *Monsieur.* "The eggs are already cold. And is that bacon crisp? It is not, by heaven! The cook must hear of this, my dear."

"Yes, yes," my mother said, with her shaking hands making vague motions toward eating. "I shall speak to the cook."

"Returning to the dead boy. . . ."

My mother whispered something, growing whiter than ever.

Here I leaped from my chair, in a child's frenzy, with my teeth set and my hands gripped tight.

"You shall not do it any more!" I shouted at my father. "You are killing my mother, *Monsieur!* You are killing my sweet mother."

*Monsieur* leaned back in his chair and

laughed at me, combed his black beard, and laughed luxuriously again.

"See, see, Julie," he said. "What a little knight your boy has grown to be. And what an excellent imitator. One touch of rebellion from Hubert Guillaume . . . and now this. Every kitten will shortly attempt to play the cat."

"Leave the table, Jean," my mother said to me.

"No, no, no!" cried my father. "He must stay. The young hero must stay. But what can he mean? Can he possibly mean that I have wounded you, Julie? No, but I see very clearly what the truth is. What was Hubert Guillaume to you? He was not your flesh. Why should you be troubled by this ridiculous fuss?"

"François! I loved Hubert . . . I . . . ."

"You must not weep," François said.

She rallied with a great effort. "I shall not weep," said my mother, while I sat wretchedly at my place, staring from one to the other, knowing that my outbreak had only made things worse, and wishing that a bolt from heaven would break through the roof and carry all that house to perdition — so long as *Monsieur* might be one of those who perished.

"We have become quite confused," *Mon-*

64

*sieur* stated, taking a good swallow of coffee and pausing to enjoy the taste. "We have quite tangled ourselves in so many little digressions. What I mean to say, in short, is that we cannot, surely, mourn for a soul that has gone to heaven."

"Indeed, no, François."

"Excellent! Then why should we mourn for Hubert Guillaume unless . . . but is it so? Do you consider him a damned soul, Julie?"

"François, in pity."

"Ah, Julie, still you will avoid me. But this is a matter in which I need your voice. We will begin by admitting that there are flaws in your education . . . that we cannot set up Julie as a universal authority. Upon one subject I dare swear that she can speak as well as any one in this world. Julie, upon this theme you should be expert . . . upon heaven, I mean."

"François!"

"Do not protest. You are a saint. And you have been given into the arms of such a husband in order that your martyrdom might be developed . . . in order that your sainthood should be well ripened, let me say, so that you may ascend to the blessed land beyond death with the full flavor. As such an authority . . . as such a practitioner of devotion and charity and all the other virtues whose names, for the moment, I forget . . . as such an authority, I really must beg of you to tell me. Could Hubert Guillaume inherit heaven, guilty as he was of so many vices?"

My mother managed to say that she knew of no great vices in Hubert and that she was sure he would. . . .

Here my father interrupted her again: "You know of none? Do you not know me? And do you not know that there was much of me in him? Tell me, Julie, are you not honestly aware that I am destined for the high court of the devil?"

"François," my mother gasped, standing bravely against this bludgeoning, "I think that Hubert Guillaume was a proud, strong soul, but a good boy."

"Julie, my love," François said with a sneer, "I lay ten myriads of thanks at your feet. From this moment my last care about Hubert is gone. I rejoice that he has left us, though so abruptly, upon the upward road. With your authority, Julie, I shall always picture him to myself as one of the saved."

He had continued too long. My mother had leaned her face for a moment in one hand. Now she settled gradually forward — like a sleepy child, one might have said

— and laid her head on her arms.

*Monsieur* snapped his fingers. "Julie!" he called.

She did not answer.

"Julie . . . I command . . . no tears!"

Still she did not speak. *Monsieur,* with a terrible face, jumped up and strode around the table. He drew her back by the shoulder, and her head fell to the side. She had fainted utterly away. All that was wonderful in this was that she had withstood the torment so long.

*Monsieur* looked down upon her for a moment. "A little too much talk of heaven," he said.

# Chapter Eight

# A Warning

The priest came from the village and found my father walking in the garden, whistling and giving directions to the head gardener. It was through him that the report of the conversation went abroad, somewhat decorated in the repeating, I have no doubt.

"I have heard of the sad loss that has come to *Monsieur*," said the gentle priest.

"You mean, of course, the suicide of my son?" *Monsieur* stated in his big, cheerful voice. "Well?"

"In such times, it is my duty to offer my help," said the priest steadily. "Will you tell me, *Monsieur*, how I may serve you?"

"Will you tell me, Father, in what do I need service?" *Monsieur* asked.

"If not you, there is your dead son," said the priest.

"He is gone," *Monsieur* responded, "beyond the reach of your voice, I fear.

Whether up or down, I cannot tell . . . if there is an up or a down. I have recently had an assurance . . . of almost professional authority . . . that he has taken the upward road. At least, I consider that subject closed."

"It shall be my privilege, then," said the priest, "to offer up my prayers for him."

"Do not do so," said *Monsieur.* "It is a peculiarity of the Limousins that they are either very well saved or very well lost. I should be grieved to have you lose your labor."

"May I ask, then, *Monsieur,* if the burial is arranged? I presume it is to be in the holy ground of the Church?"

"You presume too much. That is a question on which I neglected to ask the wishes of Hubert Guillaume. I have only the suggestions of my own mind to follow in the matter. They lead me to make his grave near the château."

"At whatever hour you choose, then," said the priest. "I shall be ready for the service."

"I thank you a thousand times," answered my father, "but in this case there will be a need for no ministration except my own. Having been partly responsible for his coming into this world, and having been partly responsible for his sudden departure from it, I shall attend to putting him under the ground without the help of any other hands."

"*Monsieur,*" said the priest sternly, "I do not wish to say it . . . but this is frightful sacrilege! For the sake of your own soul, *Monsieur.*"

"It is now twenty-seven years," said *Monsieur,* "since that subject worried me. Good morning, my dear Father."

The priest left him. Here, the gardener reported afterward, Pierre Reynal, who had been standing apart until the interview was ended, came up and said: "I have found the very spot, *Monsieur.*"

"Good," said my father. "I have been searching the grounds all the morning, and I have found nothing that I think will exactly do. Take me to the place."

Reynal guided him to a hillock just south of the château. Two huge maple trees shaded the place.

"If an avenue were cut through the woods just before us, and toward the river," said Reynal, "there would be a view of the water."

That suggestion pleased my father. In a little time, scores of axes were slashing at the woods, opening a great, raw-edged gap through them. Nearly every available man on the place and from the village was employed to follow the hewers and remove the stumps. It was a riotous, furious labor, for *Monsieur* insisted that the work should be done before the dusk.

All that long day the crowds moiled and toiled, but while the sun was still well above the western trees the thing was ended. A way had been cleft through the forest, the stumps had been torn or blasted from the rich soil, all had been raked and leveled, and now from the hillock beneath the maples a pleasant reach of the eye carried through the long avenue and across the Limousin River.

My father gave orders to Reynal and Argen to lift the body and carry it out. There was no coffin. While Hubert Guillaume lay on the grass, some workers sank the grave. *Monsieur* jumped into the pit, received Hubert in his arms, and lowered the body to the floor. After that, he sprang out again, shoveled in the soil with his own hands, refilled the grave, raised the mound above it, and in the gathering dusk gave directions that a great slab of gray stone be dragged to the top of the hill and placed on the site. This was done, and so the ceremony ended.

*Monsieur* sat down that night to dinner with my mother as calmly and as cheerfully as though he had been out hunting all the day. It is doubtful which gave him the more pleasure — the stern repression of his own emotion or the knowledge that this singular funeral ceremony would fill the countryside with talk and with horror. Although he was, of course, studiously playing a part, when I think back to that day I feel one emotion far more than all the rest — a sense of the gigantic grief of *Monsieur*.

He bore up during five or six days after this. I think that, if anything, he was more amiable, bright, cheerful, than I had ever seen him. I knew, for instance, that the loss of Hubert made him detest me. Why should his first son have been taken and such a weakling left on the earth? Yet he forced himself to show a peculiar interest in me. He even attended some of my lessons under Argen; he even walked out to see Reynal putting me through my paces on a horse. I was at that time learning to sit a trotting horse without a saddle — with my arms folded across my chest. My father watched until I slid off when the horse made an abrupt turn. He picked me up, laughing.

"Well, Reynal," he pronounced, "is he not becoming a man?"

At the end of the fifth or the sixth day, *Monsieur* suddenly collapsed. We heard a great voice rolling through the house, and Reynal went up to the third floor to find my father standing in Hubert's room with a light in his hand, searching everywhere and calling out impatiently: "Hubert! Where the devil are you, Hubert?"

He turned to Reynal when he entered. "Where can he be? Has he slipped out to go night fishing?"

"No . . . I think there is a girl in the village . . . ," said Reynal.

He managed to get my father back to his room, and then he had the courage to remain there with him, after covertly sending one of the servants after the doctor. What a picture that must have made, as the messenger hurried at fast as Thoroughbred horseflesh could bear him after the doctor. My father, staggering with fever, his eyes wild with delirium, roving back and forth through the room, asking Reynal why the devil he dared to remain there — and Reynal, like a grinning devil in very fact, sitting without a word of answer in the corner of the room.

When the doctor came, there was great trouble in getting *Monsieur* to bed, but Pierre Reynal managed it by persuasion, when the others had almost given up.

For ten days my father lay there in danger of his life. It was a fortnight after the crisis passed before he could be wheeled out into the shade of the summer day. I remember wondering at the pale skeleton of the man that had been *Monsieur*. It was said at the time that nothing could have saved him from dying except the angelic patience of my mother, who brought her own self to the verge of a collapse by refusing to leave his bed.

In fact, in the early days of his delirium, when the full measure of his giant strength was still upon him and four men could not keep him in his bed, my mother would run to the raging monster, take his great wrists in her child-like hands, and force him back upon the pillow.

Worn and weary as she became, I never saw such happiness in her as when she had the life of *Monsieur* in the small hollow of her hand day after day. For the first time, I was pushed into the background, and I began to understand the greatness of her devotion to *Monsieur*. She had married him for the purest love; to her death day, in spite of a thousand enormities, she loved him with as bright a fire as ever.

The doctors wished to send my father out of the August heats to the mountains, but he resolutely refused. In a week he was walking; by September he was nearly his former self. It was wonderful to see him come back to his full power. Only one mark remained upon him after the ecstasy of that sorrow — he had a jagged mark of silver in the hair above his right temple — on that side only, without a gray hair on the left side of his head. If his appearance had been strange and awful before, it was doubly so now.

Early in October, he came back from his first day of hunting that season. He came back in the early dusk and ordered everyone in the house to be gathered before him in the big ballroom. Lamps were carried there hastily, and everyone thronged in, beginning with my mother and ending with the lowest scullery worker. It made an odd scene.

That room had not been used since the death of *Monsieur*'s first wife. I could not think of it, far less step into it, without feeling her spirit fall strongly about me. All the windows were heavily shuttered and hung across with curtains on the inside —

all except one which had been forced open, allowing a wild current of night wind to stream in, fluttering aprons, fanning hair loose, and tossing the flames in the throats of the lamps.

"I have called you together," my father announced, "to speak to you about gambling, and particularly about card playing. I do not wish to put what I have to say upon the basis of morals. I am not interested in them. But I have a strong prejudice against gambling in all its forms, my friends. A very strong prejudice! The reasons for it I shall not discuss. The fact is sufficient. Do you understand me?"

With this he turned his brilliant eye across the crowd. It flicked across me, among the rest, and I felt that gaze sink in upon me.

"My prejudice," he resumed, "is so great that I have called you here so that everyone might hear what I have to say, while I speak in such terms that I cannot possibly be misunderstood.

"I shall not spy out your pleasures. I shall appoint no one to watch you. My direction is simply this. Do not allow card-playing, particularly do not allow gambling, to come to my notice. For the instant you do, those who have been concerned in it must leave my service, forever." He made another brief pause here and added: "Those who do not leave my service, leave my life!"

After that he dismissed them all with a wave of his hand. My mother and I crowded out with the rest, feeling not a whit better than the other servants of the house.

"Did you mark what your father said?" asked my mother.

"He seemed to say that if you or I, even. . . ."

"It was aimed at you, Jean. You are young, but you will never forget such a thing as this. If you gamble and he learns of it, Jean, you will be cut off from him . . . cut off without a penny of his fortune. He has warned you once. He will never speak of it again . . . but, if you transgress, there will be no mercy and forgiveness and no second chance. You will be ruined forever, Jean. Will you understand, dear? Will you take this into your mind and remember?"

As if I needed such a warning when the death shot of Hubert Guillaume was still ringing at my ears.

# Chapter Nine

# A Span of Years

You will agree that in the writing of recollections such as these are, nothing is more difficult than to maintain a viewpoint that is continually changing. Therefore, I shall not attempt to trouble you with what I was and what I did between the ages of twelve and eighteen. Hitherto I had done nothing remarkable, except that as a child I was able to win the settled hatred of two such men as *Monsieur* and Pierre Reynal. Another era was about to begin in which, quite outside of any desire of mine, I was foisted into a more active life. I skip at once from my eleventh to my twentieth year.

I showed you myself last, by inference as much as by picture, as a too sensitive, too femininely frail child with a meager body and a pretty face. I present myself to you again in another condition in my twentieth year.

That sinewy lover of the woods, Pierre Reynal, had made me follow him through the forest for ten long years. He had taught me to trail and to shoot, to run great distances at high speed like an Indian, to trudge on foot under great weights like a trapper, to swim, to box, to wrestle, to ride. In all of these things I had acquired very extraordinary proficiency. I do not mean that I had become a wonder to be pointed at, but I was at least far beyond an average. I had before me the grim picture of my father as an ideal to struggle toward.

I knew that I must make immense efforts if I ever expected to develop my naturally slender, light body; those exertions I made generously, keeping before myself for years the hope that someday I should grow to a sufficient bulk and a sufficient might of hand to please and astonish even my father. Fate limited me. On the one hand, it raised me up; on the other hand, it cast me down.

You have been horrified, I have no doubt, at the thought of reading of a man with a womanish face — particularly since the writer of memoirs must, with or against his will, be the hero of the tale. You will be glad to know, therefore, that fate raised me up by taking from me the delicate prettiness of my childhood. At twenty I was blessed with a good square jaw that somewhat redeemed the rather feminine modeling of the rest of my features. The matter in which fate cast me down was size.

I understand what a vastly important matter size is in a man — at least from the viewpoint of a reader. You perhaps have in your mind an ideal vision of a stalwart six-footer, big-thewed, with the arms of a Hercules — although my own observation is that a man of a hundred and sixty pounds will outwalk, outrun, outwork — yes, and outfight the majority of lumbering big men. I was not destined to attain to even such a middle size. Perhaps many of you will wish to close this book at this point when I confess that I am a little man; that at my tallest and straightest I am a scant quarter of an inch above five feet and eight inches in height. My weight never ran an ounce above a hundred and forty pounds. As the years went on, I found myself at twenty weighing just what I had been at eighteen, and the period of growing definitely ended. As I came to understand that I must habitually lift my head when I was in the lofty presence of *Monsieur,* perhaps a few of you will understand that I was sad. None of you will know the sickness of soul that was mine.

A slight man must work by sleight-of-hand and tough endurance; it was my good fortune to have a Pierre Reynal to give me both qualities. If I could never stagger him in wrestling, yet I could often flash my gloved hands past his guard as we boxed. If I could never quite attain to his uncanny skill with a rifle or a revolver, yet, when we jogged down a long trail, I at last had the satisfaction of knowing that I could run as fast and as far as he. These were great things to me.

It was a measure by which I could judge the arrival of manhood on myself when I looked upon Pierre Reynal more as a human being and less as a devil. Not that the first cold awe ever entirely departed; not that I could ever pierce through the mystery that surrounded him any more than *Monsieur* himself could. Having been with him every day for more than ten years, I had grown accustomed to his ugliness and to his silences. Sometimes I attempted to probe past his reserve.

"Why," I asked Reynal, "should a man like you, with many accomplishments, with a knowledge of men, with experience in the world, with courage and with wit . . . why should such a person desire to pass his life in an obscure corner of the wilderness?"

"That is a question, *Monsieur* Jean?" he said.

This was the usual barrier that he erected against curiosity. On this day, I whirled on him with anger. "Answer me, Reynal!" I commanded, and stamped my foot.

I was ashamed at once and expected him to laugh in my face, but he was a fellow who seldom so much as smiled — although smile he did now. He decided to give me an answer.

"If I were in Paris or London, say," remarked Pierre, "would I really be any nearer to the sky, than I am now?"

"Do you love nature so much?" I said contemptuously. "Are you a poet, then, Reynal?"

"If you consider that," said Reynal, "you will see that we are all poets, more or less."

"Bah!" I said. "Is *Monsieur* a poet?"

His hideous smile twisted his face again. "Yes . . . a dramatic poet."

I could not get any more than this out of him, and this was the greatest amount of his speaking at any one time that I could recall up to that moment. However, it satisfied me that he could talk and that under some conditions he would talk. I often tempted him, but he never grew eloquent again. This little glimpse of him renewed a thought that I had always had — that Pierre Reynal did nothing except what he planned carefully.

There was no element of the haphazard in his nature. I felt assured that his first coming to me in the woods when I was a little child was the result of a deeply planned scheme which took effect more fully when he became a member of our household. All that he did drove on toward some great end.

What could that end be? That it was a vital and a dangerous end, I had partly his demoniacal ugliness to convince me, and partly that instinct of dread which had welled up in me when I first saw him. How much that instinct had developed in me I am almost ashamed to say. Pierre Reynal could not come near to me, even hidden by a wall or a tree, without giving me a warning of his presence through an odd chill in my flesh and shortness in my breath. Others, to whom I have talked of this thing, have matched it with great tales of mental telepathy that bridged seas and lands and brought minds together. Yet I never got over the ghostly astonishment of this feeling.

How many hours I spent speculating on the ends of Reynal I should be ashamed to say. I was convinced that his presence in that house concerned me, and that in the end, therefore, I should be drawn into a frightful disaster through his means. You will say that this is the sort of prophecy that is always written down after the event. I assure you that long before the dénouement I talked of this feeling of mine to my mother, and she tried in vain to weed the thought out of my mind. She feared Reynal as I feared him, at first. A woman grows calloused more quickly than a man, however, and my mother had grown quite accustomed to Reynal.

"It is only his ugly face, Jean," she said. "What has he done, ever, to harm you or to harm any other person?"

Before I finish speaking of Reynal at this time, I must add that during the fourteen years he had been in our household, *Monsieur* himself had never dared to presume too much upon him or treat him as a mere hired servant.

Argen was a different matter. My father now despised him. I mark my own advance to manhood chiefly by the fact that while my dread of *Monsieur* and of Reynal remained undiminished in vigor, my dread of the tutor turned gradually into a consuming contempt. This in spite of the fact that, as the years went on, I found that there was a really prodigious store of knowledge in the man.

He was one of those with the peculiar ability to sweep a page with a single glance, lift the facts off it, and keep them imprisoned in his memory forever. He had read everything, and he remembered everything. His one fault as a learned man was that there was little order in his mind. As I grew older, I found that no matter in what direction I turned there was still something left to plunder in the mind of Argen. In spite of my absence from any school, I feel that my education was infinitely better than that of the average youngster of that age. All was owing to Argen.

My mother had not changed or grown older, in my eyes. I was born when she was very young, for she was married to *Monsieur* when she was only seventeen, and I was born the next year. When I was twenty, she looked hardly eight years older than I. There was not a line in her face. Her eye lighted as readily as the eye of any child. Her laughter was as sweet and as smooth. Time had brought her a little nearer to heaven, and that was all.

My father, the last of the three people who made up my life, being the greatest of all, is reserved for the last. He had aged hardly any more rapidly than my mother did. He still retained his vigor and went out on tremendous all-day marches when he hunted with Pierre Reynal. In the meantime, I had formed a comparison that, I felt, gave some clue to his nature. My reading had supplied me with the figures of Zeus and Mephistopheles. I felt that *Monsieur* could be considered a composition of their natures. So I explained him, still realizing that there was something left of him over and above my explanation.

Here, then, is all the background of my life, in brief, as I came to that day in my twentieth year when I went down to the river to meet Reynal. I found him seated with Argen under a tree — and there were cards in their hands.

# Chapter Ten

# Forbidden Fruit

I was stopped by a shock of horror while Argen, with a wretched exclamation, began to sweep up the cards and the money. Reynal stopped him. "*Monsieur* Jean is not a traitor," he said. "You need not be afraid."

"He may ruin us with one word to *Monsieur*. We are in his hands!" cried Argen.

Reynal fixed his grisly eye upon me. "You need not fear," he repeated to his companion. "You will not betray us?"

I was filled with loathing — partly at the sight of the detested cards and partly because I had found Reynal and Argen. It was as though one of the principal devils was to amuse himself in the company of a minor imp.

"I shall tell nothing," I said briefly. "And yet, I should be glad to know what makes you do this. Particularly since you know what has happened in the château. You,

Argen, are you not afraid that it will get you a cut throat?"

Pierre Reynal was not apparently offended at this insinuation. He merely shrugged his strong shoulders and said: "Speak to him, Argen."

My tutor cast a guilty glance over his shoulder. Then he held up the pack before me and flicked the cards with a whirring noise.

"Consider, *Monsieur* Jean," he said, "that this is a sad little life we lead in this world."

"Does playing with those little bits of pasteboard make it a bigger thing?" I asked, still full of contempt.

"Ah," said Argen, "that is according to the viewpoint. There are two ways of looking at a book, let us say. On the one hand it is so much white paper marked with ink. On the other hand it is the voice of Job, of David, of Homer, or of Shakespeare calling out of the deep well of the centuries."

I smiled at the eloquence of Argen. "Come," I stated. "I shall listen to you now. Let me hear you make that comparison good."

"I shall do it, have no doubt. I have only illustrated a greater thing with a lesser."

"Impossible!" I responded.

"Do you think so?"

"What is greater than Homer, then? These silly cards?"

"He was only a poet, and a poet deals only with the beauty of life. There is a greater thing in life than its beauty. There is the cruel strength of life . . . there is fate, *Monsieur* Jean."

"You cannot hypnotize me with a great many words," I said coldly. "What have these things to do with fate?"

"You are not an ignorant child. You know that some of the greatest souls in the world have loved Fortune . . . worshiped her."

"Every drunkard," I said with the rigid authority of virtuous youth, "excuses himself by speaking of the great men who have loved wine. This manner of talk does not convince me, Argen. I am only bored."

I looked away from him, across the shining river and over the dark evergreens beyond to the clear blue sky, all towered and castellated with brilliant white clouds. But, as a matter of fact, I was keenly eager to hear what more he had to say of such a mystery.

"You are bored, *Monsieur* Jean," said Argen, "and yet these little cards put a gun to the head of Hubert Guillaume and shot him through the brains."

I jerked my glance back to him, and with a wild impulse I raised my hand. The coward shrank from me, and my own scorn of him made me lower my arm.

"Forgive me!" said Argen. "Yet these things are all true. Sometimes a shock is needed to open the mind. But, in fact, *Monsieur* Jean, out of the movements of these cards there comes the face of the greatest power of the universe . . . fate, sir. It is fate that we hunt for in these games."

He said it so solemnly that I felt a shiver of conviction run through me.

Yet, I argued: "You are not hunting dollars, then? You are not simply trying to get something for nothing?"

In place of answer, Argen smiled upon Reynal, and Reynal smiled at Argen. I felt that I was pushed away from the heart of the discussion, as a child is put off by his elders when they speak of something beyond the comprehension of tender years.

"Do men go mad for the love of money? Do they throw away themselves for money? Do they sacrifice all that is near to them and all that is dear to them? Observe, *Mon-*

*sieur* Jean . . . is Reynal a light-minded man?"

It was the most convincing argument of all.

He began to manipulate the cards with active fingers as he spoke, and then he dealt, flashing the polished cards through sun and shadow in the mottled shade of the tree.

He talked as he dealt: "Here is a hand to you, my dear Reynal. I place another hand here. A third hand to myself. You observe? I pick up my own hand, a card at a time. The first card? It is a hope. The second card? My heart looks still higher. The third card? No, it is nothing! The fourth card . . . it has joined all three before it. Perhaps this fifth card will give me a wonderful strength. With that strength I shall crush the other hands, I shall run the betting to the sky. I shall see the perspiration form on the forehead of Reynal. The fifth card . . . hah! . . . it is nothing. The hand is worthless. You observe, *Monsieur* Jean."

"My hand," said Reynal seriously, "is worth a lot."

"Let us see the third," said Argen. "Ah . . . ah! What a pity, *Monsieur* Jean, that you did not hold it. You could have wagered to the skies. Ah, well." He gathered the cards into a neat pack again. "Do you begin to understand a little better, *Monsieur* Jean?"

The very fact that it was a forbidden fruit was working in my blood now. Suddenly I sat down cross-legged and made the third angle of the group.

"Deal me another hand," I said. "At least, it will do no harm for me to understand the thing. Let me have a hand."

"I?" cried Argen, the hypocrite. "Could I do such a thing to the son of *Monsieur?* In the first place, he would tear me to pieces."

"Nonsense!" I exclaimed. "Do you think that I am a weakling? Do you dream that I shall allow this thing to become a habit with me? It is no more than an experiment with me."

"Never!" Argen contradicted, shaking his head with violence.

"He is not a child," Reynal stated again. "Let him do as he wishes to do."

It would be useless to describe all of the game that followed. You have guessed it already. They had drawn me in with the utmost ease. My very contempt for them and their game made me the easier victim, and they began, of course, by allowing me to win a hand — and then another hand.

Then again! I had a few dollars in my pocket to begin with. It had swelled to half a hundred in those few instants, and I was drunk with the joy of the game.

Afterward, of course, I lost and lost and lost still again. My money was gone.

"Bad luck," Argen remarked sympathetically.

"It is the end," I said, filled with gloom. "My money is all gone."

"Ah, but your credit is good!" laughed Argen. "And in another moment you will be having a run of good luck as surprising as this run of bad luck. It is always that way. There is a balance in the game. That is the beauty of it. Is it not, Reynal?"

"Yes, of course, it is so," said Reynal.

So I settled myself at the game again.

That day the game ended while I was still a few dollars ahead. I fell asleep dreaming of the hundred hands in which a difference in one card. . . .

Every day hereafter we had a few moments, stolen here or there, but usually in the secret heart of the woods. Of course, I began to lose, and, although it was only a little, I grew ambitious. I began to plunge to make up my losses. Straightway I found myself a hundred, five hundred dollars in the debt of Argen. It was always Argen. Reynal seemed to remain about even with the game. I was the loser; Argen was the winner.

He was extremely sympathetic, but he would always say: "Now is the time that I should stop . . . while I am ahead. Because, in the long run, the chances must be equalized and you will draw even again . . . then ahead."

"Only today's game," I would insist. "This shall be the last time. You cannot refuse me a chance to recoup, Argen."

"Ah, well," he would say, "I must submit. I cannot refuse a loser."

Was it not simple?

Within a month the blow dropped upon us — out of the clearest sky. Reynal had expected the thing for some time. *Monsieur* announced on a day: "I feel that Jean has studied at home long enough. It is time that he went to a school, Argen."

"As you will, *Monsieur*."

I was struck with terror. If Argen were sent away, and if he asked me for the money I owed him. . . .

"No, no, Father," I insisted, "there is still a great store in the mind of *Monsieur* Argen, and I have barely touched it!"

My father fixed me with his bright eye.

"Has *Monsieur* Argen taught you to address me in such a loud voice?" he asked. "Then it is time for you to change masters. I shall hear no arguing, Jean. It is finished."

# Chapter Eleven

# The Dilemma

In such a time, one becomes desperate with hope at once. If I were utterly downhearted and despairing at first, I soon decided that things could not be so bad. A paltry debt of five hundred dollars could not ruin the heir to the enormous fortunes of Limousin. As soon as my spirits had raised to this point, I thought of friends.

What friends had I to whom I could appeal? The people of the household were the only ones whom I knew. My friends were our domestics! It was odd that in this condition I should think of that other man, Pierre Reynal. Yet he had money, I knew.

I determined to go to him, not because I felt the slightest friendship for him or expected him to feel the slightest friendship for me, but because I felt that even an enemy, who understood what my financial expectations were, could not but be glad to lend me money and take a handsome profit upon me, besides the advantage of gaining my sense of an obligation to him.

My interview with Reynal gave me my first direct evidence of the hatred he had for me.

"You know, Reynal," I said, "that I owe money to Argen, and that he is about to leave. I have no money to pay my debt to him, although it is only five hundred dollars. I am ashamed to go to my mother and tell her the story. Now you, Reynal, I believe to be a saving man. Surely you have a great deal of money in the bank. If you will advance me five hundred dollars, I shall be glad to give you my note for a thousand."

Reynal sighed and shook his head.

"At least," I said, astonished, "you cannot doubt that I shall be good for such an amount?"

"Good for it?" asked Reynal. "*Monsieur* Jean, I realize that to the heir of *Monsieur* five hundred dollars is less than a penny to Pierre Reynal. But why do you come to me? I, too, have played with Argen. The scoundrel has charmed the cards."

I was about to tell him that it was impossible that he should lose fifteen thousand dollars so soon, and at cards with a single man. On a moment's reflection I saw that, if he were lying to me in order to avoid paying me the money, it would simply embarrass him to tell him what I knew about his savings and force him into a greater lie on my behalf.

This refusal of Reynal's reduced my resources terribly. I knew then that it was true he hated me and wished my ruin. First of all, with despair growing, I returned to Argen.

I told him my situation, that I had not a penny of cash, that I was ashamed to ask my mother — that my father, of course, needed only one hint of the truth of the matter to ruin me instantly and cast me out of the house. To a boy who knew nothing of the world it seemed more terrible than a dragon, more awful than *Monsieur* himself. Besides, I was not very brave.

How many admissions have I made to you? Now I must confess this, also. I was no more of a hero than I was a giant, and at the thought of being thrown out into life with nothing to rely upon except my own wits, I shrank. I begged Argen to take my note for a thousand dollars and forgo the immediate payment of the five hundred.

Argen said: "Alas, I wish I could oblige you, *Monsieur* Jean."

"Is it impossible?" I muttered.

"Consider," he said, "that your violent father has already given his orders. I aim to be taken away tomorrow, presented with a ticket to Quebec . . . and so an end to fifteen years of my life. I, a man no longer young, am cast out without a resource. Is it not a sad thing?"

"Do you mean," I said, trying to understand him, "that you have no money except the five hundred dollars which I owe you?"

"I have my pay for the last month, which *Monsieur* so kindly gave me this evening. That and the five hundred dollars is all that stands between me and the poorhouse . . . and I grow old, Mister Jean, I grow old."

There is a species of hypocrisy so artfully worked that it defeats its own ends. I did not believe a word that the artful Argen had to say, but here was only one answer that I could make to him.

"Listen to me, Argen," I said. "I shall give you my note for one year, and the sum shall be fifteen hundred dollars. I shall manage to save that much from my allowance when *Monsieur* sends me to college. Surely that is good security for you. I think that any money-lender would give you at least twelve hundred dollars in cash for the note of the heir to Limousin. Is not that true?"

Argen smiled sadly. "You do not know these money-lenders," he answered, sighing. "If you did, you would not suggest such a thing."

I had not enough knowledge of the world, of course, to deny him. I simply made a gesture and raised my offer.

"Consider two thousand dollars and a year's time, Argen. I am offering you four dollars for one, and only a year to wait."

I saw that he was tempted. He started a little, and his active little eyes wavered to and fro. At length he shook his head resolutely.

"A dollar now means perhaps ten times what a dollar will mean at the end of a year."

"What!" I cried warmly. "Is it possible that you are really without money? Have you won nothing from Reynal at the game? Confess, Argen!"

"Won from Reynal?" he asked with what seemed to be very real astonishment. "Won from that fox? *Monsieur* Jean, you do not know what you say. Reynal is the sink into which all of my savings of these years has disappeared. The man is a dragon. He devours money. But go to him, by all means, and he will be glad to oblige you with such a small sum as five hundred dollars on almost any terms. For my part, *Monsieur* Jean, I weep that I am forced to be so hard on you. It is only the most frightful necessity that compels me."

The two hypocrites were determined to cast me back and forth from one to the other and so avoid me, although they had not concocted their stories any too well beforehand. For a moment, a hot wave of anger brought a stream of words into my throat. Before they were uttered, cold fear choked them away again. If I annoyed Argen, he could go straight to my father and with that. . . .

How I sat through dinner that night I cannot tell. *Monsieur* was full of talk about a new Thoroughbred that he had bought, a beautiful mare of distinguished lineage, of which he hoped the greatest things. I listened and smiled and nodded like an automaton. After dinner, my mother took me apart to her own rooms.

"Now, tell me, my dear," she said. "There is some trouble in your mind. Come, tell me all about it."

I had determined that nothing should induce me to cast such a burden of worry upon her, but, as I have admitted, I was not a very brave young man. Besides, in my ignorance it seemed that to be cast out into the world was to be cast into a fiery furnace full of tortures. In another instant I was groaning out the whole story, from the beginning, laying as much blame as possible upon the temptation that the pair of them had put in my way.

It is impossible to tell how people will react in a crisis. I had expected that my mother would break into tears — perhaps fall in a faint, and I was ready to support her. Instead, I found that there was more strength in her than in me.

"The traitors, the traitors!" she cried. "If only François himself is not behind all of this. Or if I had money."

A new terror caught hold on me. I cried to her: "You are the wife of François Limousin! Cannot you find at least five hundred wretched dollars?"

"I could not find five, I think," she responded calmly. "But there is a way in which I can raise money. Of that I am sure." She took my hands. "Jean, have you any idea of the value of jewels?"

"None in the world."

"And we have only until the morning."

"Yes. The blow will fall then. That cruel devil, Argen. . . ."

"Hush!" she admonished. "But there is a pawnshop in the town. Do you know the place, with the three gilded moons over the door?"

"I do not know it."

"You must get there tonight. You must make it by tonight. It is at the end of the main street, next to the bakery. Do you understand?"

"I remember the bakery."

"You must go there with some of my jewels and pawn them."

"Ah, and what if *Monsieur* desires you to wear the very jewels that I pawn?"

She banished that idea with a light gesture. "What is that?" she said, dismissing the notion. "What will he do to me compared with what he will do to you? If necessary, I shall pretend to have lost the whole jewel casket. If he storms . . . oh, what of that, Jean? If you are safe, I shall laugh at it. I shall laugh at it."

# Chapter Twelve

# The Jewel Man

We sat in her room, two foolish children. I cannot tell which of us was the younger or the more silly. A big lamp stood at the end of the table, and, because the evening was warm, a window had been left partly open, so that the draft made the flame of the lamp swell and die. Its reflection on the richly polished mahogany lengthened and dulled in turn. Before us, my mother placed an inlaid box, long, narrow, deep, and so heavy that she settled it on the table with a jar. It was very ancient, but the inlaid coat of arms was still bright.

Then our eyes were lost in the treasures of the jewel box. It was very large, as I have said, neatly fitted with trays, one below the other. My mother took them out and arranged them before us.

"Ah!" I cried at the first sight of them. "Here is enough to buy another Limousin!"

"Do you think so?" my mother asked, frowning in thought. "But I wonder? Are you sure that you know nothing about the prices of these things?"

"Nothing whatever."

She picked up a necklace of pearls which lay in her transparent hand like distilled moonshine — moonshine that gleams through a thin, silver land mist. "What could the value of this be?"

"I could never guess. I should think . . . a fortune."

"But there are imitation pearls, Jean. Oh, yes, I have heard of such things. You had better take this. And here is a. . . ." She dropped the necklace into a bag of chamois skin. She selected in turn an unset ruby, bright as the eye of a dragon. It filled the whole palm of her hand with red lightnings.

"This, surely, is not a sham," I insisted.

"Alas," said my mother, "I cannot tell. You must be sure to take enough. For, oh, Jean . . . if you should fail . . . if François. . . ."

"Hush," I warned, growing eager as I saw deliverance before me. "You must not think of it. Only tell me, dear, how you can forgive me?"

She merely looked at me with such love

that my heart ached to think that such an angel should have been put upon the earth among men. Now she swept a whole handful of gems into the bag.

"Take these, at least," she said.

I accepted a bag heavy with wealth. The least gem of all and the tiniest pearl in that necklace was worth twice my debt to Argen, as I had occasion to learn afterward. Yet when the bag was in my hand, and I looked down to it, it seemed impossible that out of this little bag could come my deliverance.

Hurrying to my room, I dressed for riding and went out to the stable. The groom who was on night duty jumped up and stifled his yawn at once.

"Let me have Prince Charlie," I said. "And quickly, quickly!"

"But Prince Charlie has not been ridden for a fortnight. He is very wild."

"What is that to me?" I asked in anger. "I want a horse under me with legs tonight."

He hurried off. On second thought, I went after him, and together we saddled Prince Charlie. He was quiet enough until he smelled the saddle; then he began to quiver and dance, hungry to be out and flying. Before I mounted, I looked at the man as I had never looked at another human being, thrusting my inquiry through his startled eyes and into his soul.

"If a word of this night ride becomes known . . . ," I began.

His eyes opened a little wider, and then he tried to smile. "Ah, *Monsieur* Jean. I am discreet."

As Prince Charlie carried me through the door of the stable, like a lightning bolt rushing out of the dark of a storm cloud, I thought I saw among the trees to the right a tall shadow of a man — Pierre Reynal.

The road through the estate wound in a leisurely fashion, but there was no leisure in my blood that night. The excitement of Prince Charlie was in me, and my nervousness was making him burn. I drove him like a winged arrow through the woods. We whipped over fences, plunged through low-branched coverts with me lying along the working neck of the stallion. Finally we cleared the last barrier and straightened out on the highway that led to the town.

The soft going through the woods had hampered Prince Charlie's speed. Now, with firm footing, the ring of his gallop was like the roll of heavy musketry. A low moon hung in the west, with the wind whipping clouds across its face — the wind and the rush of the stallion. Although he plunged and shied at every shadow, I had no fear of him. There was a greater fear within me, and, besides, Pierre Reynal had imparted to me some of the magic by which he ruled the brain of a horse rather than its mouth.

I could not let the Prince fly all the way. After a time, I took him back to a more moderate gait, but still we were driving fast when the stones of the village street clanged underhoof, and I drew up with a clatter before the three gleaming moons of the pawnshop.

I tethered Prince Charlie and went in past windows crammed with great, foolish-looking jewels such as would take the eyes of the townsmen on the one hand and fit their purses on the other. At the clatter of the bell, as the door closed behind me, the broker came hobbling from the rear of the shop, raising the lamp in his hand to see me the better. I hardly saw his face — only the bright and snaky glitter of his eyes as the lamp was raised past them.

"And now, sir?" he asked in a harsh voice.

"I want five hundred dollars," I said, abrupt with eagerness. "Have you so much money in your place?"

He fumbled at his ragged mustaches and his goat's beard — I suppose to cover his smile.

"Five hundred dollars," he stated, "is a great deal of money. A great deal of money, my friend." He shook his head at me. "However," he went on, "a great deal can be managed when there is the proper security . . . excellent security. What have you there?"

I opened the bag. "I do not know what you will think of these things," I said, shuddering with anxiety. "But here is one. Is it worth much?"

It was a chain of delicately woven gold, weaving as fine as wool, which supported an emerald as broad as a man's thumbnail, cut in a thousand glowing facets. The hand of the broker darted out like a bird's claw and scooped up the treasure. It could have purchased his store, all that was in it, and his hope of salvation besides. He held it under the light, and I watched the quivering of his fingers. I have no doubt that to him it was a glimpse of heaven.

"Has it a value?" I asked.

"Ah, well," he said, "imitations all have a value. They are amusing, unless they are really as badly done as this."

"Is it an imitation?" I asked. "Then I

shall take it back."

His hand closed hard over it. "The chain has a price . . . a small price," he insisted hastily. "What else have you to offer?"

I produced a handful of rings from the chamois bag. Each was a gem worthy of a rich man's collection. I remember in the lot a black opal set with points of golden fire, and the broker took them one by one. He drew in his breath as though he were drinking.

"I have made no mistake. You are *Monsieur* Limousin's son?" he said.

Will you understand why I hesitated an instant before I answered? I hardly looked upon *Monsieur* as my father. He was a god or a devil — a power and a danger — but as my father?

"Of course . . . of course!" I hastened to answer as he lifted his thoughtful eyes to me.

"I cannot say that I am interested in these things," he said. "But as trinkets they have a certain value . . . a certain small value. Have you anything else?"

"Yes," I said gloomily. "But I suppose that nothing will please you."

I poured the entire contents of the bag on the counter. He surrounded that heap of dazzling wealth with both his arms and uttered a faint moan of wonder.

"Ah!" I cried. "*This* pleases you!"

The broker gathered his senses slowly. "Unfortunately, *Monsieur*, it is all very poor stuff."

I was only a child — or little more. I cried: "Then I am lost! But return it to me. . . ."

"Wait," he commanded. "I have little time to be troubled with these things, but because you are the son of *Monsieur* Limousin . . . as a favor to the family I will. . . ."

"No! My father must not know of it!" I exclaimed.

He rubbed his scrawny hands together, nodding and grinning. "Oh, I am not a fool. I am not a fool. I am a man to be trusted. As for these things . . . give me the bag. I shall put them away . . . and you will have your five hundred dollars."

He took those priceless treasures and began to write out a ticket.

"I cannot write out the list of all these names," he said. "We will secure the money . . . let us say on this little ring, shall we not? As a joke between you and me."

"Very well . . . whatever you choose. But quickly."

"Patience! Patience! You will have the money all in due time. Patience."

His hand trembled and stumbled as he scratched out the ticket of receipt. As for his intention, there is not the slightest doubt of it. He had acknowledged only the receipt of a single gem, although even that little ring was worth twice the value of the five hundred that I was to receive. As for all the rest of the gems in that unlucky chamois bag, he intended that no Limousin should ever have a glimpse of them again.

Then I heard the galloping of a horse in the street.

"What is that?" I exclaimed to the broker.

He lifted his evil ear in alarm. "And what could it be, except a rider?" he said. "And as for the. . . ."

Here the galloping horse — and it was driving at full speed — came to a halt before the very door of his shop, and the next moment that door was cast wide by the towering form of — *Monsieur!*

# Chapter Thirteen

# A Premonition

After that first glimpse of him, I assure you that such a whirl of black blurred my eyes that he was jumbled with the dim outlines of furniture, lamps, and the cringing figure of the money-lender who saw fate stride in upon him inopportunely.

My father merely said to me: "And how are the manners of that rascal Prince Charlie, Jean? Have they improved?"

Luckily for me he did not wait for an answer. I could not have spoken if an angel of the Lord had come down and stood at my shoulder to give me courage. *Monsieur* walked straight past me and towered above the counter.

"Ah?" he said.

The pawnbroker cowered and tried to smile. "A little joke," he gasped out. "A little jest between me and young *Monsieur* Limousin."

The long arm of *Monsieur* went out, and his hand seized upon the chamois bag that the wretched man had not yet recovered presence of mind enough to put away from him. My father poured the contents upon the counter.

"What was the sum?" he asked at last.

"*Monsieur* . . . the point of the jest . . . the five hundred dollars. . . ."

"And this is your security?"

"I intended to return all those things with my own hands to *Monsieur* in the morning. But . . . in the hands of so very young a man . . . and at night . . . for the sake of *Monsieur* I felt their safety could be more trusted in the safe of. . . ."

My father turned his back upon him and started for the door, saying cheerfully to me: "I think it is time that we started on back. Is it not?"

In some manner I managed to get through the door of the shop and into the saddle, and then we went back to the château through the night. There was not a word said. Sometimes, as I turned my frightened face toward him, I saw the big outlines of *Monsieur* as he rode down the way. Sometimes I heard him speak pleasantly to his horse. All the way my terror grew, while with a fumbling brain I strove to construct my story, and found nothing to construct. There was no lie on which I could put my hand.

When we came to the stable, the groom, with a face like death, came to take the horses. One look at him was sufficient assurance that he had not betrayed me, but now he was to lose his place — and he was a man with a family to care for. He had been more than twenty years with my father.

*Monsieur* was whistling as we started toward the house. Before we reached it, he wheeled on me suddenly and said: "If you have made up your mind to a story, tell it to me now, Jean. As well tell it to me now."

"I have nothing to say," I assured him.

"Nothing? Well, well, what a limited imagination you have, Jean. Or can it be that you are simply a coward?"

He scratched a match and held it up. Behind that quivering tongue of yellow flame I could see the steady brightness of his eyes, like the eyes of an animal. I endured it as long as I could and then put up a hand to shield me.

"*Phaugh!*" breathed *Monsieur*, and with a snap of his fingers he tossed the match away into the dark. He went in before me, saying in perfect contempt: "You had better go to your mother first. She will be naturally curious, Jean."

I went to her, of course, and when I tapped at her door, it opened to me at once. She was wrapped in a bathrobe, and I could see that she had not gone to bed. She drew me in and closed the door with a guilty quickness behind me.

"You did not get it, Jean?"

"No."

"And the jewels?"

"*Monsieur* has them."

I stood before her like a beaten dog with my eyes at her feet. When her silence made me look up to her face, there was no scorn in it, only pity and terror.

"Does he know anything?" she said.

"I have not told him."

"What shall we do, Jean? Oh, if I were a man. What shall we do?"

"We can only wait," I told her.

"We must not fold our hands. There is some way to fight back. Oh, Jean, for my sake think of something . . . for if the blow falls on you, it will kill me!"

I went to my room in a trance of despair. I knew it was very likely that my mother had not exaggerated — in crushing me, *Monsieur* would be crushing her, also. But, although I told myself that I must think of her, plan for her, struggle for her, between me and my brain's working came the wretched thought of myself.

Have you ever faced yourself? Is it not true that in the days of your life you have never faced crises that reached to the bottom of your soul and made you aware of the reality of all that you are? Is it not true that the self you know is a pleasant dream? But I, during that night, stood face to face with my naked self, and the picture that I saw sickened me. When I think of the change that came afterward, I do not attribute it so much to the shock and the catastrophe as I do to the long time of agony that had preceded the falling of the blow. It is the well-plowed ground that produces the surprising crop.

The morning came, miserable, dull, hooded with gray fog. I crept early to the room of Argen, and I told him with a sick voice that I had failed to secure the five hundred dollars with which to repay him.

"Ah, ah, ah," murmured Argen, as if the news cut him to the very quick. "How terribly unfortunate."

"But whatever happens," I said, "it cannot be that you will tell my father. For you understand that it would be my ruin, Argen, and the death of my mother . . . for the sake of five hundred dollars."

"I shall at least promise you this," said Argen. "I shall not speak to *Monsieur* on this day."

"But tomorrow, Argen? If you intend to strike me, strike now . . . it is the frightful suspense that kills me, and that kills my mother, also."

He said with irritation: "Why did you ever draw her into the thing? Why should she know anything about it? Well, I shall only promise that I shall do my best . . . I shall do my best for you, *Monsieur* Jean. If only I were a prosperous man . . . but you know that I am a pauper and five hundred dollars to a pauper. . . ."

I left him knowing that nothing could be affected by a further appeal to him. His mind was made up, and in the meantime I had only the wretched assurance that I was free until the next day. Argen left that morning, and Pierre Reynal accompanied him to the town at the suggestion of *Monsieur*. When I heard those orders given, I wondered again if my father were not the heart and the head of the plot himself — if he were not the source of all this Machiavellian scheming? I began to lose all care for myself in a growing concern for my mother.

It was her last twenty-four hours of life. There was a dreadful premonition in me that death was close to her, and that she was to die for my sake. I swore to myself that I would find a way of preventing the trouble from coming to her. I went to her as happily as I could after the departure of Argen and told her that I was safe; that Argen had sworn to me that he would not reveal a thing to *Monsieur;* that I was to have ample time to repay my debt to him. As for the explanation of my presence in the pawnshop to *Monsieur,* I would soon be able to think of something effective.

She seemed as ready as a child to close her eyes to the danger and look upon the more cheerful face of the situation. We spent every moment of that last day together like a pair of lovers. I paddled her through the limpid shoal waters at the edge of the Limousin River. My mother sat among cushions at the bow, following the rhythm of my laboring strong shoulders with worshipful eyes. Then she would look down to her hand that trailed over the side, leaving a shining furrow in the lake. With all the craft that Pierre Reynal had taught me, I made that canoe glide as silently as a wish. There was only the bright flash of the paddle now and again as it was half unsheathed from the water, and the sun struck a flare from it.

I felt, as the canoe moved on in that magic silence, how like a child's was the pure soul of my mother; how dreadful was the fate which had given her to *Monsieur.* I understood why she could love him and, indeed, love all who were around her. It was owing to her inability to think of herself. If there had been no one around her, she would not have existed; in her fear of others and her love for others was her whole soul.

When the prow touched the sands, at last, my mother sighed: "Why have we not done this before, Jean?"

"We shall do it a thousand times hereafter," I said as I helped her to the beach. At this, she looked up to me, without sorrow, but with much thought in her clear eyes. So a child lifts its head.

"Do you think so, Jean?" she asked. "Have you a premonition, dear?"

The wind out of the damp forest blew through me the chill of other worldliness.

"Why will you speak in such a way?" I said to her.

"Does it seem a little ghostly?" she

asked, smiling. "Perhaps it sounds foolish to you, Jean, but I am full of the feeling that you will never take me out on that delightful river again." She turned and looked back across the river. "Ah, Jean," she continued, "how sad I am that there is not a clear sunset on the water this evening."

I could not endure it any more. I caught her in my arms, and with a trembling in my throat I begged her not to speak like this again.

"Dear silly boy!" she said, and patted my cheek.

But the horror would not leave me. When we came to the edge of the woods and looked out on the château, I put my arm around her and drew her back.

"We must not go in for a moment," I said.

She looked up at me and then at the great château where the lights were being kindled and the windows were turning into soft rectangles of yellow mist. Someone was playing the piano — perhaps it was *Monsieur*. It was in his strong, tumultuous style.

"It *is* lovely, is it not?" she commented, smiling on me.

"Do not go in," I repeated, with that unearthly grief and foreboding swelling in me. "Oh, my dear, I feel that if you go in now . . . I cannot say what I fear. But don't you feel as though there were strangers living in the château? As though we had been away from it for many years, and now we do not know who may be in it?"

"No, no, Jean," whispered my mother. "You must not say it. It has been in my mind so many times. But now . . . it is time to change for dinner, Jean. We must not be late . . . we must not, Jean. Not while your father is suspicious and hostile toward you."

"Only five minutes more. Let us stand here, quietly, until the lights are all kindled. See, there is a breaking of the clouds in the west, and a little red and gold comes through."

"Yes, Jean. And see how it turns the tower windows into flame!"

"Dear. My dear," I murmured, "do you know how I love you . . . how tenderly and how sadly I love you, my sweet mother?"

"Why, Jean . . . why, Jean . . . you are so serious. And why sadly, Jean?"

"Do you not understand?"

She swayed a little toward me. What a flower-like and fragrant thing she was!

"I dare not understand, Jean."

# Chapter Fourteen

# The Letter

My father, at dinner, was ever so gay and full of charm; he was particularly bent, it seemed, on drawing Reynal into the conversation. Therefore, he turned the talk much upon horses. Although *Monsieur* knew almost all that a man can learn about horses, Pierre Reynal knew them by instinct, and that is the better knowledge. But who could make Reynal talk? No one, I am sure, in the whole wide world. *Monsieur* had striven before, with compliments, to make the soul of Reynal warm and so to open his lips. Still he never succeeded, nor did he on this occasion.

However, he was so gay and so talkative, as he tried to execute his scheme, that my mother now and again smiled and nodded a little upon me as though to say: "You see, everything is not so bad. *Monsieur* is forgiving you . . . and all will be well, Jean."

Today, perhaps, yes. But after that evening?

What was *Monsieur* saying?

"That old fellow, Argen . . . was he not odd, my dear Julie? Was he not odd?"

"I presume he was, François."

"See," said *Monsieur,* waving to my mother in a mock admiration, "is it not noble? She will not admit a shadow of suspicion even toward a departed man. Ah, Julie, how little schooling you will need from the angels.

"This Argen, when he left Reynal at the train, gave him a letter for me . . . a letter which I was requested to leave unopened until tomorrow, but I am a curious fellow . . . as you know, Julie. I could not resist opening the letter this evening. A queer letter, Julie. A queer letter, Jean. Will you let me read it aloud to you?"

He pulled it from his pocket and shook out its folds. He was eating olives, slowly, so that the reading of the letter required an amazing length of time. I, knowing that the devil was now unleashed, strove to reassure my mother by smiling at her, but she was already tense. Reynal, on the other hand, kept that expression that never changed — the hideous leer that the drawing scar kept upon his features.

"He is a gay rascal! Consider this opening . . . 'My dear *Monsieur* Limousin. One leaves with regret associates which have endured through ten years, or nearly for that length of time. No, it is more! But in your company, *Monsieur* Limousin, one loses consciousness of a great deal except *Monsieur* Limousin.' "

Here my father paused to enjoy another olive.

"What can he mean by that?" asked my mother.

"Have patience, my dear Julie. Perhaps we shall learn in due time."

He spread out the letter before him so that I could not help seeing that all the letter consisted of was perhaps half a dozen lines scrawled across the paper. My amiable father was merely doing a little improvising before he settled to the actual contents in the hand of Argen.

He began again. "'And as I leave you, *Monsieur,* I cannot help giving to you in writing a confession which I could not make to you in person before I left the château. Upon my honor, *Monsieur,* I shall leave you with much sadness. And the confession that I make is that I was never happier than when I was in your house.

" 'Does this, perhaps, seem odd to you,

knowing as you do that a man of culture rarely finds pleasure in the position of a domestic in any household? It was because of the novelty of that household, *Monsieur,* that it was possible for me to remain in your company during the ten years.' "

Here he paused again to take another big, ripe olive, nibbling it with much delicacy and smacking his lips a little to get a more pronounced flavor out of it.

"What do you think of this letter so far, Reynal?"

"Why, it is a letter," Reynal agreed, in his casual manner avoiding any expression of opinion.

"And you, Julie?"

"It seems a very polite note, François. I do not think *Monsieur* Argen is quite as odd as you make him out."

"We are still only in the beginning of this letter, my dear. Let me continue. 'What most entertained me, I cannot say, where everything was amusing. In the first place, I was always entertained by the tyranny of *Monsieur* himself whether it was politely restrained . . . or whether it was brutally open, knocking down people right and left.' "

"François!" broke in my mother.

"Well, my dear Julie?"

"Is it possible that any man in the world has dared to speak to you in this manner?"

"Wrote to me, Julie, not spoke. Be accurate, my dear. However, let us continue. 'But on the whole, *Monsieur,* I never knew whether I was more revolted or entertained by your wicked treatment of *Madame* Limousin.' You see, Julie, that you do not lack some champions, even dumb ones."

"It is really impossible . . . the thing cannot be!" said my tormented mother.

"I give you my word. I have not misread a single syllable. It continues in this fashion . . . 'As for *Madame* herself, a sheep always makes one think of a wolf, and I have sometimes wondered if the submission of *Madame* to your brutalities was not the cause of the brutalities themselves rather than an essential cave-man element in *Monsieur*'s nature.'

"And what do you think of that for scoundrelly impertinence, Julie?"

"I cannot tell what to say," said my poor mother. "It is bewildering to meet with such treatment from one who has been in one's house for ten years."

"Is it not?" *Monsieur* said, smiling upon her while he fumbled in the dish blindly for the largest and the firmest olive. "But to continue . . . 'There was the delightful Reynal, also. I could not dismiss him without a word. Is he aware that he is a mystery? Is it a clever pose, carefully maintained, or is he simply stupid, like, let us say, *Madame* herself?'

"What do you say to that, Reynal?"

Reynal said nothing. The color in his cheeks did not vary a trifle.

*Monsieur* continued with his improvisation: " 'Which brings me to *Monsieur* Jean. I leave him with regret because he is such a docile pupil. And there are possibilities in him that perhaps you, *Monsieur,* have overlooked. Let me call to your attention that the quiet rogue is often the effective rascal and that personal courage is not always necessary to a life of crime. I warn you, *Monsieur,* seriously. And it is to give body to my warning that I add what follows.' "

"I shall not listen!" broke in my mother. "The dastard! The coward to strike such blows after his back was turned."

"Was it not cowardly? However, I think it is interesting, also. Let me continue . . . where was I? Let me see . . . yes, yes . . . here it is. 'You are aware, *Monsieur,* that the use of cards has been forbidden in your house for some time, since the death of your unfortunate elder son.' "

I knew, now, that he was reading the letter that had actually been written, and to which he had chosen to add such a stinging prologue. I dared not look at my mother. I could only stare fixedly across the table toward the inscrutable face of Pierre Reynal.

" 'I regret to say that *Monsieur* Jean and I have broken that prohibition and have played for some time recently, until *Monsieur* Jean found himself some five hundred dollars in my debt. I mention this with regret, and only because I leave you penniless, or nearly so. And five hundred dollars to me is a very great fortune. Translate it into terms of food and shelter and you will understand me, I am sure. *Adieu, Monsieur.* Your obedient servant . . . Argen.' "

Long preparation for some trials often makes the trials themselves more unendurable. I was tensed to brittleness, and the blows of *Monsieur* crushed me utterly. Now he folded the letter slowly and turned his eyes upon me.

"Rise!" *Monsieur* ordered.

I stood up almost like one under hypnosis.

"Say one word. Say yes! Or say no! And say that word only! I am not in a humor to listen to a plea. If Argen lied, he shall die.

If he has spoken the truth. . . ."

"*Monsieur* . . . ," I began.

Here a pitiful cry from my mother broke in. "François, will you not let me tell you how he was tempted and. . . ."

"I do not wish to hear from you. I am speaking to your son. You, it seems knew all about the matter some days ago. And in spite of that knowledge, you kept the word from me, Julie? Is it possible that you have deceived me?"

He stood up in turn. How he towered above me. He was in such a mighty rage, and his fury had so grown upon him during the restraint of his improvising that now he was trembling and quaking.

"Speak!" he shouted.

I could only mutter: "It is true . . . only. . . ."

"How could you have been so weak, Jean? Even a fool and a coward should have the wits to know that such an estate as mine is worth some restraint. You should have used temperance, Jean. You should have delayed until the estate was in your hands, and then you could have aired your true self . . . your true, pitiful, shameful self. You could have indulged your secret vices. You could have filled the château with gamblers, tricksters, and cheats. But you were too hasty, Jean. You rushed upon your fate too blindly, Jean! Do you know it now?"

His voice swelled to a frightful violence in the last dozen words, and he made such a gesture that I shrank away from him and threw up my hands to shield my face. As I did so, such an expression of scorn and fury came into the eyes of *Monsieur* as I trust I shall never see again in another.

"I have loathed you from your infancy!" he said between his teeth. "I have hated you from your childhood. I have detested your pretty face, your girl's voice, your sneaking ways. That Hubert Guillaume should have been taken from me and such a thing as *this* left in his place!

"Leave me, Jean. Leave the château. My part in you I renounce forever. My eye shall never rest on you again. Go quickly if you love yourself . . . and never come in the reach of my hand again or. . . ."

I had already withdrawn some paces before his thunder, and now my mother ran in before me. She caught at the raised hands of *Monsieur,* and clung to them.

"François!" she gasped out. "Will you hear me? Will you . . . ?"

He brushed her aside, not violently, but the strength seemed to run out of her body, and she slipped lightly to the floor. I tried to catch her, but there was nothing firm for my arms to receive. She lay with her eyes closed, whispering: "Mercy, François. . . ."

Then her eyes opened, and a faint smile touched the corners of her mouth. I knew that she was dead.

# Chapter Fifteen

# The Reincarnation

I raised her in my arms. She had no more weight than a bit of air, and I carried her past the silence of Pierre Reynal, past the white horror of the butler. *Monsieur* came before me at the door, but I lifted my eyes to him and brushed him aside with a glance. I carried her under the lofty dome of the stairwell, past the two armored knights who guarded the first step on either side with their foolish halberds. I passed the stained-glass window on the first landing, and the Italian Madonna on the second. The thick carpet of the second floor turned my steps to a whisper, and with that whisper I carried her into her room.

The moon was there before me and, falling through the window, dropped first on the clustering, transparent petals of a vase full of lilies, then fell along the rug and brought out dimly the Persian colors.

Yonder lay a light wrap thrown over a chair, with its folds dropping gracefully to the floor, and a pair of gilded slippers stood beside it — a silver wrap and golden slippers, in that light. The air was delicate with the fragrance of the lilies, her favorite flower.

I laid her on the bed and turned from her, for it seemed to me that there was more of her in the breeze that came from the west than in the body that lay behind me. I had a strange illusion that she had at that moment finished dressing, turned down the lamp that burned low like a watching yellow eye from the corner, and hurried from the room. She was on the deeply carpeted stairs, now — she was passing the Madonna, the light from the strong lanterns which *Monsieur* kept burning at night outside the stained-glass window fell across her and robed her with the wings of a splendid butterfly. She hurried past the rigid watchers at the bottom of the stairway . . . she entered the dining room. . . . She found the three men standing rigidly as I had last seen them. The white-faced butler, the silence of Pierre Reynal, and *Monsieur,* stupefied at the door. All the house had fallen into silence. Neither was there the slightest sound from the forest, not so much as a whisper.

I closed the eyes of my dear mother, kissed her lips, and then, because I could not cover her face without breaking my heart, I drew the curtains around the bed.

I think that there was less grief in me then than I had felt in the evening when we came out of the edge of the wood into view of the château. Then the foreboding of all this had come over me so strongly that death itself was hardly more than the accomplishment of a prophecy.

It was hard to pass through the door. Twice I attempted to open it and step back into the hall. Twice I knew that when the door was closed I, who was still within a step of her, would be an eternity away.

I was weak, nearly fainting, when I stood in the hall at last, but I had a passion inside me that brought back strength. It flushed me with heat and sent me running to my room. There I tore off my dinner jacket, and I dressed for the woods.

Sometimes great emotions make the mind strangely clear. I could name to you now every detail of the clothes that I donned, how I hesitated for some time between two hunting coats, how I took high shoes that laced almost to the knee because, as I told myself, they would do either for riding or for walking, and how I selected a strong corduroy hat, a stout flannel shirt, comfortable gloves. Under the coat I strapped a new cartridge belt with a holster hanging at the hip. Then I went to the stock of guns. They had never interested me greatly, except as textbooks interest most boys. They were merely a part of the long and often tedious lessons that I was forced to take from Pierre Reynal. At that instant they became of the most overwhelming significance, and I went over them, one by one. I passed over everything until I came to an old Colt. It had a lucky feeling to my hand, and I thrust it down into the holster with a certainty that this was the weapon for me.

I was seething with a terrible fury. The Greeks believed in avenging Furies; they were in me on this night, so that I did not even pause to consider the strangeness of my new self.

When I was equipped in this manner, I went downstairs and threw open the door into the dining room. All was as I had expected to find it. *Monsieur* and Pierre Reynal sat at the table. The plate of Reynal was covered with untouched food, but *Monsieur* had eaten with a good appetite.

Now he looked up to me and smiled at his companion.

"See, Reynal," he said. "My romantic son is about to rush forth into the night, but if. . . ."

I closed the door and hurried out to the stable. The news was already there. They hurried in anxious quiet to saddle the horse I called for. Then I mounted and rode past the western side of the château, so that I could have a last look up to the open window of my mother's room. After that, I spurred wildly away.

A fine, hard animal was under me, but as I spurred through the night, it seemed to me that the poor beast was resting between every stride. In the gray of the morning, it stumbled and fell dead beneath me. I left it without a backward glance and went on through the wet forest; a chill sprinkle of rain had been falling for the last hour. So, dripping, I came out on the sight of a village.

It was well into the morning, now, and the breakfast fires were dying. Over a dozen houses there was only a thin ghost of smoke, lagging feebly to the side, soon eaten into nothing by the falling mist. Suddenly I was very hungry. I felt in my pocket for money, but with all my care in my departure, I had not taken away a penny of money.

As I read the last few pages I see that there is little more than a recital of bald facts to give you an idea of the change in me. When I found myself without money, my remedy for the evil seemed the most natural thing in the world. I turned up the wide, wet collar of my hunting coat over the lower part of my face, turned down the brim of my hat as far as I could. Then I stepped into the first saloon.

The bartender was doing a thriving business for that time of the day. He had just set up a round of ale and was rubbing down the bar, laughing noisily at the last joke. There were half a dozen men in the line that faced him. First they stared at him as his laughter stopped, then they followed his fixed eyes to the gun in my hand. They were like so many automata. I had pulled a string, and all their hands went up. I made a gesture with the muzzle of the revolver that sent the barkeeper from behind his bar and backed him against the wall with the others, their arms thrown stiffly above their heads.

"Hello!" called someone from an inner room. "What's made you all so sad?"

I smiled to myself as I backed around

the bar, pulled open the cash drawer, and put the contents in my pocket with my left hand, while I studied their faces calmly over the hand that held the gun. They were as obedient as so many children. I backed out the door again, then whirled and leaped for the back of the first horse that stood under the front shed of the saloon with thrown reins. I sent one bullet through the door of the saloon to discourage an immediate pursuit, and in fact I was almost a block away before those seven brave men stumbled out into the street, frantically yelling and waving their guns.

That pony, which I had chosen at haphazard, ran like a Trojan to the next town, nine miles west. By that time the rain had ceased. The day had turned warm, and there was only a thin sheeting of gray across the sky as I stepped into the restaurant.

A red-faced, plump girl, wearing a dirty, white apron, came from the back of the little room.

"It's too late for breakfast, and it ain't time for lunch," she said pertly.

"It's *my* time for lunch," I replied. "Get me something at once."

And she did. I sat there and ate with a

grave deliberation, as though I were not aware that fifty horsemen were pounding down my trail by this time. That thought gave me only a mild tingling of pleasure and not the slightest apprehension. I knew that my strength had come upon me; my old self lay dead with my mother in the Château Limousin.

# Chapter Sixteen

# A Note from Monsieur

When my pursuers reached the town, they came with a crashing that filled the village street. While the waitress ran to the front door, I finished my coffee, took my coat over my arm, and walked out the back way — walked, I repeat, hardly knowing whether or not I desired to have them overtake me. They did not.

They were still milling around the restaurant when I came to the station where a westbound freight was going out. I swung aboard it and climbed an iron ladder to the top of a boxcar, where I sat down and looked about me. A brakeman came running back along the tops of the cars, pouring out oaths. When I gave him a handful of silver, he sat down beside me.

"I figgered you for a deadbeat," he said

with a strong American accent, "but I see you're just a gent out for an airing."

If I say that this was the first happy day of my life, you will understand that it was not because I was insensible to the death of my poor mother, but because that death had taken place in another age, long before the birth of my new self. That new self sat with a joyous heart on top of the train of empties that whirled west at a dizzy rate. In the evening I dropped off at a little town and took a room at the hotel. There a deep fatigue swallowed me up, and I dropped into a heavy sleep without taking off my clothes. That turned out an excellent thing, in the end.

I was wakened by a repeated knocking at the door, and a voice calling.

"Limousin! Jean Limousin!"

I wondered, then, how my name could have been known, for the one I had written on the hotel register had been out of a book — I forget what it was.

"Yes?" I said, noticing that the gray of the morning was just beginning. At the same time I realized that, if they knew my name, it was because they had followed on my trail.

"I have an important word for you, Mister Limousin."

"Very well," I replied. "Let me get on

some clothes, and I'll open the door to you."

"Never mind that. I must see you at once!"

There was a threat in the ring of that voice now. By the stir of feet I knew that there was more than one in the hall. I glided to the window; my room was only in the second story of the building, but there was a sheer drop beneath me. There was nothing left but the door. So I jammed my hat on my head, took my old Colt by the muzzle, and, turning the lock, threw the door open.

"Enter, my friends," I said.

Then I stepped to one side, so that, as the door swung open, they had before them only the gray gloom of the dawn, very dim compared with the lamp-lit hall.

A big man strode in with a gun in his hand, saying as he stepped: "I arrest. . . ."

I struck him down with the barrel of the gun, gave the next man my fist with a force that split the skin across my knuckles, and hammered the heavy gun into the face of the third. If you have seen the effects of a Colt when it is clubbed, you will understand why I was not troubled as I ran lightly down the stairs. There were only groans left behind me, and then the stamping of fumbling feet. But by the time the hotel was roused, I had taken to the woods.

My intention was to make a long detour and come back, the next morning, to the line of the railroad, which I could follow up until there was a convenient chance of getting aboard a freight train at the first sharp grade. I marched steadily that day with very few pauses until, in the evening, I shot two squirrels and made a fire to roast them. It was dark before I finished my meal, so I made a bed by the fire and was prepared to stretch out on the evergreen boughs, when a shadow stepped out from among the trees.

The harsh voice of Pierre Reynal said: "It is a friend, *Monsieur* Jean. Do not be alarmed!"

My old self was not so dead that the sight of the monster did not send a chill through me, as before. But there was too much hatred in me to permit fear to be the ruling emotion.

"I am not alarmed," I said coldly. "But why are you here?"

He seemed in no hurry to reply, but, with his hands on his hips, he looked up to the dark rising of the trees above us.

"This is a very snug corner, *Monsieur* Jean," he said. "I see that you have remembered some of my lessons."

"Reynal," I said, "I wait for your message."

"It is from *Monsieur*."

"Very good. Has he not said enough? Did he forget certain ways of condemning me that he wished to send by your mouth?"

"*Monsieur* has sent me to beg you to return to him, *Monsieur* Jean."

Callous as I had become, I was struck weak with astonishment. "He has sent for me?" I repeated vaguely. "*Monsieur?*"

"Yes."

"On what peculiar conditions, Reynal?"

"He has made no conditions. He has sent me to beg you to return."

"That is a likely story," I commented. "And particularly likely that you would have come for me even if he sent you. Do you think that I have been blind to you, Reynal? Do you think that I have not seen that you hate me and hunt me down? Do you dream that I am not fully aware that you, Reynal, played into the hand of that rat, Argen . . . or he into yours, which is more likely . . . to drive me from the château? And by the same token, it is you who have helped at the murder of my mother!"

My fury took me by the throat. "Ah, you devil!" I cried. "If you have come like a man to fight as a man should fight . . . then I welcome you, Reynal. Here are the woods. There is no witness. You are armed, and I am armed!"

Reynal said gravely: "I shall never fight with you, *Monsieur* Jean."

"Could nothing raise the man in you?" I said. "Not even this?"

I struck him across the face with the flat of my left hand. I was ready for the draw of his gun the next instant, but, although he staggered under the blow, he merely raised his hand and wiped away a drop of crimson from his mouth.

"That," he said, "wipes away part of my debt to you, but not all of it. For I confess that I have been guilty, as you suspect."

"Will you tell me, then," I said, "what fiend possessed you? Will you tell me, Reynal, what has made you hate me? Unless you saw from the first that I hated your ugly face."

He made a sudden grimace that passed for a smile with him. "As for my face," he responded, "it is the curse under which I was born. I could not blame a child, or even a man, for dreading me. As for the reason behind the things that I have done, I hope that the day may come before my death when I can confess to you. That time is not now."

"You admit that you have conspired against me?"

"I admit it, *Monsieur* Jean."

"That it was your scheme to drive me out of the house of my father?"

"I admit it."

"You admit that my mother has died as one result of your devilish work?"

"I admit that also . . . for which may God forgive me. I cannot even ask your forgiveness."

"Still, Reynal, you ask me to speak patiently and gently to you . . . as a friend."

"I do not ask that. There is your gun. I have taught you to shoot straight. Here I am, and I shall not dodge. You may pay your score against me now with the pressure of one finger, *Monsieur* Jean."

"Do you mock me?"

"I speak to you out of the fullness of my heart, only."

For an instant I almost believed him, but the least moment of reflection, of course, convinced me that it was only another proof of his strangely effective craft of mind and tongue. Yet he was not altogether such as I had seen and heard him before. Surely, in the fifteen years of my knowledge of him, he had never spoken so much in any day.

"And having admitted all of this," I said to him, fighting back the passion in my heart, "do you expect me to trust you, Reynal, and return to my father with you?"

"I have no such expectation. I have brought this letter to you."

"From *Monsieur?*"

"Yes."

I took it, more filled with wonder than ever. It was short, and, although the contents were surprising enough, yet the wording was characteristic of him in many ways.

*Dear Jean:*

*The devil who uses me as a dwelling place has done a bad bit of work, my son. I do not extenuate myself, Jean. But I ask you to come back to me and let me prove that I understand you are a Limousin and a man.*

*This is from a lonely man,*
                 *François Albert Limousin*

*As for the foolish things that you have*

*done since you left me, I shall arrange that no harm comes to you from them. There are ways of closing the mouth of the law with a secure muzzle. I am familiar with all those ways and able to use them.*
*F.A.L.*

I crumpled the letter and dropped it into the fire.

"Is there no answer, then, *Monsieur* Jean?"

"What answer should I send?" I asked savagely. "If the devil admits his wrong, is that a reason why I should come back to him?"

"*Monsieur* Jean," came the surprising reply, "I have not attempted to persuade you. I have repeated, merely, the words of *Monsieur*."

# Chapter Seventeen

# A New Champion

There was enough implied in this remark to make me wonder at that grotesque more than ever before.

"You take me back to the days of my childhood," I said. "I begin to gape at you again. But when you return to *Monsieur*, tell him that I hope a curse will. . . ."

"*Monsieur* Jean!"

"Ah?"

"Do you speak of your father?"

It was a rebuff delivered in as gentle a voice as he could manage, and I felt the injustice that was in his words.

"I am ashamed," I admitted to Reynal, "but you tell him that I am living at last, and living happily. My days with him at the château are part of a bad dream, and I have wakened. Look, Reynal. I have been a child and a weakling. But now I have strength. The end has not come yet. I am filled with it to the tips of my fingers, and the world shall feel it. I have been crouching in corners . . . I have been afraid to lift my head. Now I am my own man. Ah, I could almost bless the day that has freed me from my father. I have been myself . . . I shall be free and be myself forever!"

"Pardon me, *Monsieur* Jean. Do you not mean that you are now only a part of yourself?"

"Well, Reynal, what is the riddle?"

"You have been, in the past, only the son of your mother. Now you are only the son of *Monsieur.*"

I could not answer him at once. The truth of it came slowly home to me.

He said: "It is his own son whom *Monsieur* has recognized in the things you have done since you left him. When he heard that the horse had been found lying as it had fallen, ridden to death. . . ."

"Then he was in a fury?" I asked. "It was a favorite mount of his."

"No. He said to me . . . 'Find the boy, Reynal, and bring him to me. He is himself . . . he is my son!' As for the other things, they were so much more to him. Everything you have done has pleased him since you left the château."

Truth strikes like a hand upon a bell, and the certainty that Reynal was right now went ringing through me. It was as though a convict went from the prison with a shaved head, in stripes. That thing that I had loathed in *Monsieur* and fled from, I had taken with me, locked up in my heart. I sank down on the pile of evergreens with a groan.

"Tell *Monsieur* when you see him," I began, "that I can pay him only one compliment. When I feel the new self rising in me, I shall know it is the devil and take it by the throat, for I shall know it is his part in me. Go, Reynal, go! I must be alone."

The moon walked slowly up through the eastern trees while I sat there. As I watched it climb, I felt that it could not find in that night's journey a more miserable wretch than Jean Limousin. For all that the strange Reynal had told me was of an inescapable truth. If I hated *Monsieur*, then I must necessarily hate the Jean Limousin who had been revealed in the last day or two and whose exploits had pleased me so much.

Out of these thoughts the decision came that I must withdraw myself and live like a hermit in the wilderness until I had, at last, adjusted the double nature in me, and crushed *Monsieur* out of my very soul.

I started on my march again with the first of the dawn, having dozed an hour or two before the morning began. A shadow moved behind me, and I turned in time to see the tall form of Pierre Reynal following. I waited for him to come up.

"Reynal," I said, "I have no doubt that *Monsieur* has paid you quite well, indeed, for trailing me and spying on me."

"Upon my honor, *Monsieur* Jean . . . I have left the service of *Monsieur*."

I was staggered again, because once more it was very difficult to doubt the truth of what he said. Yet I managed to say with a sneer: "Upon *your* honor, Reynal? That will have a great weight with me, indeed."

"I am sorry," Reynal said, looking humbly down to the ground.

Thinking he was mocking me, I was on the verge of striking him as I had struck him before. But I was so assured that he would not strike back, that my hand was tied. Nonresistance in an ordinary man is apt to be like nonresistance in a dog, but a gentle tiger — a shrinking bull. There was something horrible in this new and humble air of Reynal. I cannot tell whether it angered or frightened me most.

"You have brought me the message . . . and not in the service of *Monsieur?* For whom, then?"

"For you, *Monsieur* Jean."

I flew into a child-like rage and shook my fist in his face. "*Monsieur* Reynal, *Monsieur* Liar, *Monsieur* Devil, let me tell you one small thing. If I find you again in my path, before me or behind me, I shall draw a weapon and attack you. And I shall not miss the mark. Let me tell you, Reynal, there is something in me now that will not let me miss the mark!"

"It is the soul of *Monsieur*," Reynal stated.

I cried out at him in horror, and, turning on the forward trail, I bounded off through the woods at full speed.

In the early morning I came back to the line of the railroad, and I was soon on another freight, bound west. You will believe that after my last experience I did not stop off at more towns. Only at little way stations I made a pause in order to buy a bundle of food. Then I struck west again by the first train I could find.

The life of a hobo was much simpler

then, than it has become since that time. A little money discreetly spent with brakemen gave me the range of the trains freely. I made excellent time out of the lake region and across the vast, solitary plains of the continent, the train moving like a ship through the sea.

I am tempted here to draw upon my imagination for bits of adventure and suspense to throw in at this point, but truth is simpler and easier. I have noticed that a single lie will cast a shadow over the brightness of a thousand truths. I was in danger only once, which was when I ventured into a restaurant in a little railroad town far west. It was after dark, and I felt that after putting so many hundreds of leagues between me and the château there could be little danger in sitting at a table and eating a meal prepared by other hands.

So I took a corner table, turned my back to the door, and had advanced far into the heart of a steak when a broad hand dropped on my shoulder. I looked up into the wide, brown face of a man who looked like a farmer — and something more.

"You are Jean Limousin!" he said.

So well had my description been spread before me.

He had his other hand at his hip, and I knew that a gun was in it, but I did not hesitate. I think that I was more irritated than frightened. He was a large man, and I was small, but the lessons of Pierre Reynal were in my arm and the heavy need made my fist a club of lead. I struck him down and started for the door with a dozen men, who had heard his voice and watched my response, rushing after me. Perhaps I should have been able to dart out into the night and escape without further trouble, had it not been that someone at the side of the long, narrow room threw a chair in my path, over which I tumbled heavily.

Here, I think, there might have been an end of me and my story, but, as I struggled to my feet under the very hands of my enemies, a tall man, whose face was lost in the shadow of a wide-brimmed hat, stepped into the open doorway. He had a long, gleaming revolver balanced in either hand. At his first shot the pursuit recoiled with a yell, and I leaped past my deliverer to the street.

In five minutes I had dropped the last noise of shooting and shouting behind me. I cut back to the railroad line again, and before morning I was rolling westward once more. I knew, as the freight train swayed along, that the shadow of the tall man's hat had concealed the ugly face of Pierre Reynal. It was another poser for me; since, if he wished my destruction, he had only to leave me to the hands of that angry crowd who knew me for a horse thief and a robber.

When one is traveling, one is apt to leave thought itself behind one. I left the remembrance of this scene — the more easily because I was ashamed of having run away and leaving my rescuer to face the mob single-handed.

One night I spent in a boxcar, but the intense cold awakened me. When I could endure it no longer, I pried open the door of the car and jumped out. The train staggered away around a bend and left me in the narrow throat of a valley with forest-covered mountains lifting to the snows and the skies on either side. The air was cold, but the sun was bright. It rolled in upon my spirit like a wave upon the shore. This was my country!

The last noise of the train had panted away in the distance, and the last humming was gone from the rails when I started on again northward into the woods. Although the air was as sharp as ever, and I was cramped and weak from the long, hard journey, I could not help whistling as I walked. When I was warmed with walking, and my wrist was supple, I managed a pair of very neat shots at two squirrels. In a nest of rocks I made my first mountain fire. There I roasted the squirrels and made ready for my breakfast when the sound of a rolling pebble made me look up the hills and down again. I saw my Nemesis walking toward me through the trees — tall Pierre Reynal, a broad hat on his head, a pack strapped to his shoulders. He was dressed like one who has spent all his days in the mountains. Yet I knew that he must have dropped off the same train that brought me to this place.

# Chapter Eighteen

# Strange Comrades

Anger takes to itself many strange forms of expression. I felt that I would break out in thunder at Reynal if I did not actually do what I had promised — draw a gun and warn him to defend himself. Then I remembered how he had saved me that night, and I said to him quite cheerfully: "Reynal, you have come late, but just in time for breakfast."

"I have brought some additions, however," Reynal said in a tone more matter-of-fact than mine.

He was a miracle at the selection and building of a pack. When he unfolded his kit, he seemed to have provisions for a month in it. However, the squirrels were already roasted, so we contented ourselves with crackers and coffee from his pack, taking water from one of a hundred rills that worked down the mountainside from the snows above.

"You will see, Reynal," I said at last, as he lighted his pipe and I my cigarette, "you will see that I am frank . . . I do not pretend that I understand you. I ask you to tell me why you are here. I do not even ask you to explain what freak made you save me that other night at the restaurant. But only why you are here . . . like a skeleton at my feast."

He digested the insult with no change in expression. "I am here, *Monsieur* Jean," he said, "to do what I may in your service."

At this I laughed loudly. "That is very kind," I assured him. "You are here not for any hidden reasons, not in the pay of my father, but only to serve me?"

"That is true."

"I had rather have a dog to help me!" I cried.

He made no reply.

"Very well," I said, "then make up your pack and follow me no closer than six paces."

I started up and struck north through the mountains, at a round pace. I have said that Reynal himself had made me enduring on the trail. That day I made a terrific march that must have been forty miles over that rough country. In the dusk I made a halt, and Reynal staggered in behind me. Burdened as he was by the heavy pack, what agonies he had endured to keep pace with me, I could guess from his white face. Again I wondered: *What could his purpose be?*

I said: "There is game in the woods. Find something."

"It shall be done," he said, going off with a reeling step.

I built a fire, with many a strange thought coming between me and the play of the flames that arose. Then I heard the report of a gun, and presently Pierre came in with a mountain grouse. On that we made our supper, and under the trees we bivouacked. I had not spoken a syllable to my companion since I gave the first cold order to him.

In the morning I tried him again with more than I thought any human being could be expected to endure.

"You will leave your pack here, Reynal," I said, "and go down for supplies. I intend to live by hunting through these mountains. For that, we will need several rifles, plenty of ammunition, suitable clothes and shoes, flour, bacon, coffee, and other supplies, as well as a pair of horses strong enough to pack up the supplies and good enough to ride after they have arrived."

I wanted to hear him break out in scorn and mockery. Instead, he merely replied: "*Monsieur* Jean, I may not leave you unless I am sure that I shall find you again."

"When you return," I assured him, "I shall be here. On what day will you come?"

"In nine days, *Monsieur*."

"Do you know this country, then? Do you know the nearest town?"

"I do, *Monsieur*."

Was there a subject in the world of which he did not know something? As I had directed, he did. He left his pack behind him and went off down the mountainside immediately. After that I took the pack on my own shoulders and set off on an eight-day circuit. By the end of that long march I had selected a place that appealed to me as a site for a camp — and never was there a happier journey than this lonely one of mine through the mountains. It seemed to me that in the pure mountain air I breathed out and purged away the darkness of my old life. At some other time I might go down to the cities of men, but, in the meantime, the mountain quiet was like rest to a weary man.

On the ninth day I made my camp at the spot where I had left Reynal. Not that I expected him to return in fact, because I was certain enough that he had simply gone to the railroad to return to *Monsieur* and give him all the tidings of me up to the present moment. Yet, in the heat of the mid-afternoon, I heard the neigh of a horse on the slope below — the short, stifled neigh of a hard-laboring horse. Presently I saw Reynal approach, leading two fine animals, each with a great pack heaped upon its back. I was dumb with wonder. I was even more struck mute when I saw the contents of those packs. All was the finest quality that money could buy — from hunting knives to rifles, from axes to small steel traps — and there was all that one could think of requiring in a summer camp, not forgetting a few volumes of books, chosen with an intimate regard to my own tastes — a Molière, a Montaigne, a Shakespeare, things which may be read a thousand times without weariness. Well enough. I would certainly take it all.

When I had finished examining every-thing, I said: "*Monsieur* is liberal to me with his money."

At this a suggestion of a flush appeared in the tanned cheek of Reynal. "You are unjust, *Monsieur* Jean," he said. "He has not borne a penny of the expense."

"It is your charity, then, Reynal?"

"It is your command, *Monsieur* Jean," he parried.

"Ah, well," I said. "From this moment I shall surrender. The profundity of your art surrounds me. It is a net that I cannot break through. I think that you have guided fifteen years of my life, Reynal, and I feel that I shall never escape from you. Very well, then, Reynal. Tell me what I am to do next?"

"*Monsieur* Jean will have his jest," Reynal said, sighing.

And that was all.

After that I was too busy with a new existence to spend much energy wondering at Pierre Reynal. I shall only say that in the march to the site I had selected for our cabin, in the hewing and squaring of timbers for the shack, in the raising of them with the help of the strength of the horses, in the daily hunting and cooking — in a thousand small things — Pierre Reynal multiplied himself with an industry and a handcraft amazing even to me. Beyond his work, it was his attitude that was a constant marvel, for he carried himself with enough dignity, but he seemed to have no will except my will. He was my servant, my slave, I might almost say.

We lived together through many months, but I may say frankly that these months did not help me to a clearer understanding of Reynal. For one thing, it is true that we had little actual conversation together. In the day, during the summer we hunted — one taking the rifle and the other remaining to work at the cabin, dressing skins, cooking, doing the little things that would make existence more comfortable. In the night, I took a book, while Pierre Reynal worked on chosen bits of hard wood with his knife, turning them into various images. He even constructed an intricate ship's model of consummate delicacy during the winter.

Through summer, fall, winter, and spring we remained in the cabin. Reynal went down in the fall and returned with a great array of traps, so that, when the snow covered the mountains and the furs became prime, we were ready to make a new kind of a harvest. Winter was like autumn or summer before it, except that it was brisker, more strenuous, and, indeed, more cheerful, I think. When we wakened in the morning and the hand of the bitter cold was prying at me, I used to wonder how long we could survive in that season and in that wilderness. But when one came in from the traps, yonder on the rough shoulder of the mountain went up the smoke of our fire and the proof that we were still existing. Out of that consciousness grew an exultant feeling of strength.

People have asked me if, after the sheltered life in the château, that year in the mountains was not like a prison sentence. I could always assure them that, compared with the freedom of the mountains, the château was a place of dreary darkness. There was nothing for us to pucker our foreheads over except the cut of the air when we went out in the morning, or the problems of the traps. The snowshoe work turned us into iron men, and the cold, sweet air was a friendly enemy that kept us healthy.

It was a good life in other ways. Except in storms, the round of our traps was not arduous. We never worked them with the scrupulous care of men whose prosperity for the next year depends upon them, but rather as a sort of excuse for our odd existence. We had plenty of fresh meat, always, and Reynal had laid in such a supply of provisions before he sold the horses for the winter, that he had every means of cookery at hand. And that cookery of Reynal's! He had the genius of a frontiersman and a Frenchman combined, for the production of tasty dishes.

Outside of the daily joy of stepping from the door of our shack into the presence of the great white mountains, there was only one touch of excitement during the winter. That was when a small snow-slide crashed down the mountain slope in March. We heard a rumble, felt a quiver of the earth, and then with a sound, quite resembling that of thunder, the cabin was buried.

We dug our way out and found that only an arm from the main side had shelved our way. The main avalanche would have scooped us up and dumped us, powdered fine, three thousand feet down and several miles away in the bottom of the valley. As it was, we had a week's work making a trench to the door of the shack and clearing the great burden of snow from the roof. After that, our cabin was more of a cave than a house, and we were snug, indeed, through the rest of the cold season. Although the lower world had thawed and begun to turn green in April, we were still in the white heart of winter when chance gathered us back to other men.

# Chapter Nineteen

# Duplicity

I was yawning over a book and cursing the stinging wood smoke from the fire while Pierre Reynal equipped his ship's model with cables in the form of coils of stout twine, giving her lines and ropes with fine linen thread. I, who had seen the laying of her keel and the fitting of her stout masts, felt a singular intimacy with that thing of beauty. When I was in the cabin, it was a dainty toy. When I was away, it filled my mind with the picture of a great ship at sea. I had risen to poke at the stove in a futile way when a hand rapped at our door, and Pierre opened it upon my father.

There was a powdered fall of snow that evening, and *Monsieur* came in, brushing it from his shoulders and stamping it from his feet. I gave him no greeting, but turned savagely on Pierre.

"It is your work, Reynal," I cried, "that

has brought him here!"

My father, closing the door behind him, raised his hand. "Justice, Jean . . . justice," he said. "Reynal has had nothing to do with it."

I said to him coldly: "Your word, *Monsieur,* puts it past argument."

I could tell by his faint smile that he was immensely pleased with himself, and his eyes were shining like a boy's. Indeed, I have never seen a man on whom fifty years, and more, sat so lightly.

"Courtesy, courtesy, Jean," said *Monsieur.* "Courtesy is the thing, always! You must not forget so much . . . of the good training of Argen."

I shrugged my shoulders, and then, dropping my hands into my pockets, I looked him up and down. I was full of my own strength — full of confidence — full of the bitterest hatred for him. Yet how frightfully difficult it was to meet that bold black eye.

"You have come here for some purpose?" I asked him bluntly.

"You are deliciously logical, Jean," murmured *Monsieur.* He drew in his breath through his teeth as he smiled at me. He had taken the only comfortable chair that we had been able to improvise. As he stripped off his gloves, he looked meaning-fully at Pierre Reynal. "We shall talk whenever you are ready, my boy," he concluded.

Reynal pulled a cap over his head and left the cabin at once. I was sorry for that, for, when the door closed behind him, I found that my heart was beating fast. Any man seemed to me an ally against *Monsieur*. One would have thought that he realized my growing tension, for he looked about him with a sort of cheerful curiosity.

"How well you have done it!" he congratulated. "How well you and Reynal have managed this affair of the cabin. Cold as the devil, I thought at first when I saw the snow heaped over you . . . but really this stove keeps you snug, eh?"

"Perfectly," I answered. "And now, *Monsieur?*"

"Will you sit down?" He pushed forward a stool to me with such an air that suddenly he became the host and I the interloper.

Will you understand me when I say that even that brief moment had so stamped him upon the room that it would never be emptied of thoughts of him? I felt that I should have to do something quickly, find some means of putting myself in motion.

To remain quietly there was to allow the tremendous incubus of his will to settle down upon my spirit and crush me utterly. Abstractedly I took the stool and sat uneasily upon it.

"You have changed, Jean," he began in his gentlest voice — and how insinuatingly soft it could be. "Yes, you have changed. Let us have more light." With this, he pushed the lantern a little forward on the clumsy table so that the glow fell strongly upon me and left him more securely in the shadow.

It was a trick I understood at once, but, although I felt the pressure of that light like the burden of a thousand eyes, I was helpless against it. I could not with any dignity restore the lantern to its former place.

"Changed from a boy, now I find you a man! Ah, Jean, that is often a sad time for a parent, but not for me."

My rage at this silken hypocrisy made me shout: "Do you not understand, *Monsieur*, that it is all clear to me? The mist is swept from my eyes, if it was ever there. I know that you have always hated me! Come, let us be frank and breathe the pure air. It is better."

"Yes," he agreed with a gesture of his

open hand, "you are right, Jean. And that is why I have come to you tonight . . . to lay my soul bare before you. And then to ask your forgiveness."

In spite of my years of knowing and dreading him, in spite of my certainty that this was all consummate sham, this touch of sorrow in his voice, this suggesting of resignation in his face, made emotion fill my throat. My only hope lay in closing my ears to his voice. Yet how could I do it?

He continued: "It was because I did not understand you, Jean . . . and the qualities which I loved in your dear mother. . . ."

A great shudder passed through me.

"Forgive me," he said, leaning a little forward. "When I saw them in you, I thought that you were not a man. Ah, Jean, Jean . . . am I not to be pitied a little? Pitied for my very brutality, my blindness? It was only by losing you that I could come to know you."

"Do not speak of me . . . but of her. Of her. For myself I forgive everything. It is not worth a gesture. But for her?"

"As truly, Jean," he said, "as truly as though I had taken a club in my hand, I struck her to my feet and killed her."

That dreadful picture came blindingly upon me, and I pressed my hands across my face. Yet his voice like sweet, soft, organ music ran in upon my soul.

"And for that, Jean, I am cursed forever! There is no hope for me. Shall I tell you how her sad and gentle face looks in upon me in the black of the night?"

I had never wept for her. Now the tears came up in thrilling anguish from my heart. I closed my teeth against a sob, but it broke from me. I cried like a helpless woman.

It was the hand of *Monsieur* on my shoulder and his deep voice at my ear that called me back to myself.

"Then you will understand, Jean, that out of even me something good might grow. Something from her remains in me and works in me and will never let me rest until I have redeemed myself with you. So I have begun to have a great vision of a future in which I make you richer and greater than I myself have ever been . . . of pouring vast power into your hands, which you will use only for the purest good when I am gone. I am filled with it . . . I burn with it, Jean! It has brought me west, hundreds of leagues, to find you. But tell me that you may learn to forgive me, my son."

I had turned weak as water. The very sound of his voice shook me, and, although

I submitted to him, it was really to the thought of my poor mother. I shielded my stinging eyes from the light and, looking down, answered: "Ah, *Monsieur*, I have no power against you. I cannot forget that you are my father. Do not ask me to forgive you . . . it is done already."

He stood behind me, but the sudden grip of his hands passed a tremor through me.

"This is a golden day for me," *Monsieur* said. "I shall not dwell upon it too much, or else I should be unnerved. It means that a spirit comes back into my life. Ah, Jean, when I have you back with me . . . a man! . . . what will we not do together? There has been only one Limousin . . . and yet the world has felt me. Now there are two. Shall I tell you the first great scheme which came to me for building up your strength?"

I hardly heard him. I was carrying my warm, light burden through the hall, between the two forms in armor, past the sad Madonna. . . .

"First there is the rounding out of the estate . . . all that northern district to the lake which belongs to Gerardin . . . first we shall include all of that, and how? Ah, cheaply, cheaply, Jean . . . by a means no more costly than a marriage."

174

At this I lifted my head from my dream. "I?"

"You, Jean? Sell that sensitive soul of yours for a mess of pottage? Wed you to a girl whom I have never seen . . . not even I, although the negotiation has gone so far? No, no! It means simply a formal commercial alliance for me. She is young . . . she is barely seventeen, I believe, or nineteen . . . some such matter. She will soon be trained to quiet ways in the château. She will not interfere with our lives, Jean . . . yours and mine. . . ."

Something of what followed I did not hear, this word had so stunned me, and the thought of another woman in my mother's place — a child, too, married to a man of middle age.

"But nothing could be completed," he was saying when I made out his voice again, "unless I had you at the château. The girl, being young, and probably a fool, had heard the rumors which went around the country. Rumor is wildfire . . . and it has been burning my reputation. Some truth, and a vast fiction. They have dimly traced the death of poor Julie to me. They have traced to that, also, this wild career of yours, and made that career ten times more dreadful than it is. They have written you down man-slayer and desperado . . . absurd! Marcia Gerardin, who is little Antoinette's aunt and guardian, would have concluded the marriage treaty simply enough . . . but here Antoinette raised monstrous objections. I could only prevail upon her to accompany her aunt to the château and there learn for herself what a monster Limousin is. That consent wise Marcia wrung from her niece. They are coming, but, when they arrive, Jean, you must be there. They must see that we are true father and son . . . that I am no ogre . . . that there is true love between us. And so the bird will be caught."

He laughed, and I knew that he was combing his beard with the old exultant gesture.

"As for the Gerardin lands, they will be open, instantly, to our exploitation. We shall turn a few score thousands into a million, or quite close to it. So!" A loud snap of his fingers here. "Is it not beautiful, Jean? Has it not the supreme beauty of simplicity?"

I was quite recovered by this time. At least, if I was still half unnerved, I could look easily through his duplicity, for the manifest reason that brought him west to me with that sad story was love of money, and no more.

I stood up before him. *"Monsieur,"* I said, "you have very neatly succeeded in stealing my wits away from me entirely. But not quite."

# Chapter Twenty

# Treachery

He did not rush into a tantrum. He merely looked thoughtful and muttered his first conclusion aloud: "I have been too hasty." After that, he looked at me with a sigh; I could feel that he was rearranging his ideas. "It is not to be through my love for you, Jean?" he asked. "It is not to be through this that I may persuade you home to me?"

I managed to smile, a very wry smile. "It is not to be," I said.

"I am sorry for it," murmured my father. "I had thought that the truth . . . the naked truth . . . would touch you and convince you . . . that the soul of Julie, your mother, seeing and understanding how I strove to make amends through you to. . . ."

Stopping him with a gesture, I said: "I do not wish to become violent. No, *Monsieur,* you have brought too many great, sad thoughts to me tonight. But only on one point you must understand. I do not know how long you intend to remain here, trying to persuade me, but I know that you must not speak of her again."

It whipped angry little spots of color into his cheeks, but he controlled himself with an effort that made the perspiration stand on his forehead.

"It is true," he said, "that no one is worthy of taking her name in his mouth. Very well, I shall respect that scruple of yours. But I beg you, Jean, to be open to gentle persuasion."

Here I broke out in disgust. "I shall say only one thing. You are to bring home a new martyr to the château. To you it is business . . . to me it is the work of the devil!"

"Very terse . . . very pointed," *Monsieur* said with that smile that I had long dreaded more than anything in this world. "It makes me understand that I must show you another phase of this situation. You must understand, Jean, that so long as you are rambling wildly here and there, dipping your hands into the pockets of other men, the odium of it comes back upon me. You have smudged me with soot long enough. It is not Antoinette . . . little rattle-brain . . . who has heard the stories of you . . .

the whole world has heard those stories. Now, Jean, listen to me and mark me."

"I do, sir."

"Very well. I know those men whom you have injured. I have a perfect list of those who have lost money . . . horses . . . and the rest. A prompt distribution of hard cash in varying amounts will put this scandal to bed and let it die peacefully. I can do this and restore you to your place. So long as there is no prison taint attached, your little fling at freedom will merely be amusing . . . it will make your personality more poignant . . . it will give a tang to your dullest speeches . . . if you are still capable of dullness, Jean."

Here he paused and smiled at me again; the old dread of him was tingling in my heart of hearts. I could have faced any other man, any other danger in the world more bravely than most on that day, but the terrible will of *Monsieur* crushed me and made me a coward. I felt that sick weakness coming upon me. I fought against it. My strength was already half gone.

"You will come back, if I choose," went on *Monsieur*, "dressed with a romantic reputation which does no young man harm. You need stay at the château no longer than my wedding day. And when you have given that your countenance, you will be free. I assign you, on that day, an ample allowance . . . shall we say five, ten thousand a year? Yes, or more! You will find that I am not niggardly . . . you will name your own terms. All of this, Jean, I shall do for you if you will come home."

I saw that this persuasive offer of hard cash was his last peaceful effort. Force waited around the corner of his thoughts.

"You have done harm enough," I said. "I cannot help you to do more."

"Well," he said, "I have failed. I did not dream that there was so much strength . . . of sentiment in you, Jean. Now let me persuade you with another sort of logic. I have said that it is a daily death to my reputation and an added barrier to this marriage that I have determined upon, so long as you go freely through the world according to laws of your own. I have decided that it must stop. Tonight I have brought with me three men of the mounted police. They are waiting on the mountainside for my signal. If your answer is not favorable to me, I swear to you, Jean, they shall take you. To prison with you, and not a penny of mine shall go to help you!"

What would one think of in such a time?

I was armed; my eye was sure; my hand steady. Yet, if I strove to break away from the door, the light would be behind me, and the mounted police do not miss. If I did, indeed, break through, it would only be at the price of a life or two. I could submit to *Monsieur* — temptation had me by the throat. I closed my eyes against it and said: "They may have me. I shall never help you to crucify another woman."

"Young madman!" exclaimed my father. "Look at me and listen to me, Jean. I give you still a chance to speak like a person of mature sense. Have you in mind the crimes that are charged against you? The resisting of arrest . . . it goes hard with such cases . . . would mean some years in the penitentiary. Beyond that, there is horse stealing, a heavy offense that would mean a long term to serve as soon as you had finished your first short one. That is not all. There is robbery and burglary at the point of a gun. Fifteen years, Jean, fifteen years of misery for that offense alone."

Misery in truth. I, who knew the Château Limousin, realized what a prison could be. I saw twenty-five years of my life surrendered to a long agony next to which death would be a single, simple pain. Yet, by mustering my strength, I managed to shake my head and gasp out: "No!"

Ah, how the poison worked in me.

He said: "And for what, my dear, foolish young martyr? To keep a bubble-brained girl from becoming the wife of François Limousin? Is that such a frightful destiny? Do I ask her to share the life of a criminal, or do I drag her into poverty? Is not the gift of my name like the conferring of a title? Do I not lift up that pale blood of Gerardin and blend it with a famous strain? And you, for participating in this frightful crime, what you are condemned to? To freedom, Jean! Yes, my boy, if you cannot learn to love me, then you will be free to carry your hate from me where you will . . . to Europe, to build your life newly there, gather your books and your horses and live in the leisure of a gentleman. It is this that I offer, Jean. On the other side . . . the long horror of the prison, Jean . . . the frightful shame which eats away the soul . . . the brutality . . . the darkness."

"No, no!" I screamed at him, wringing my hands together. "It is too much! I cannot do it!"

"Why, lad, you cannot, of course, of course. Because you have sense," *Monsieur* said. He held out his hand, and I saw through the mist of my agony that it was quaking a little. "Will you pledge your bare word to start for the château within seven days?"

I took his hand. It was hot and wet and closed feverishly over mine with a grip that threatened to snap bones.

"It is enough, Jean. I trust you as I would an angel. You are bound to come to me. Here is means for your travel . . . and means to appear at the château, again, like a gentleman's son. I shall not stay another instant to torment you, my boy. I shall only ask you to remember that I turned to force only at the last . . . only reluctantly."

His words came like the chime of a distant bell, without meaning. From the door I heard him call: *"Adieu!"* Then he was gone.

I was thrusting aimlessly at the embers in the stove when Pierre Reynal came in. I said drearily: "You have won, Pierre. You and *Monsieur* have won. But he has told you, of course, that I return in seven days."

The sharp cry of Reynal made me forget my grief and the cold taste of my shame. I looked at him in amazement. Here was the stoic, the Roman, turned white, clutching at his breast like a dramatic actor in a death scene.

"But not to the château, *Monsieur* Jean!"

184

"Where else?" I asked, gaping feebly on him.

A groan came from Pierre Reynal that tore even my heart. When the mute complain in a murmur, it is more terrible than a scream.

"Is it true?" he muttered. "Then there is a curse on me." He rushed back into the night out of which he had just come.

All that this implied I unraveled slowly for myself in the hours that followed. I had ample time to guess vaguely at a thousand things and come to no understanding of any of them. I could only know that Reynal had never been the blind servant of *Monsieur,* or never to such a degree as I had fancied. What the motives were, then, that had lain behind his actions and the long trail that he followed as I came west, I could not dream. Besides, there was too great a burden on my heart. Without the problem of Reynal, I had enough to occupy me.

He did not return that night. In the morning I made a circuit of the mountainside. The last of the snowfall had not buried the tracks, and I could see where *Monsieur* had come and gone again. I could see where Pierre had gone back and forth until he ran the last time straight out into the forest. Of the police with whom *Monsieur* had threatened me there was no sign whatever. He had lied.

At another time I should have raged at his treachery; I should have doubted the binding strength of an oath that he extracted through such craft. But on that day and for many a day thereafter, my spirit had fallen to such an ebb that I merely smiled at this last proof of his treachery. If he were a devil wearing a human form, he was more to be hated than despised. And what should be said of me? A villain, also, but only a weaker one.

Now that I have told so many odd and sentimental facts of myself and of my life, will you believe that I have always hated bathos and sham? Yet I shall risk telling you another thing — during the seven days I remained in the cabin, I took up a gun three times, determined to put an end to my wretched life. And three times, cursing my cowardice, I put it down again.

I told myself that it was fate. I told myself that, if Reynal were there and I could gain one scruple of moral support from him, I should have the courage to break the word that I had pledged. Again I told myself that it was fate. I made a strange vow that, if Reynal returned to me, I should not leave the mountains. Still it was fate that Reynal did not come.

On the seventh day, punctually, when the sun rode high at noon, I made up a scanty pack, took the well-filled wallet that *Monsieur* had provided for me, and walked from the cabin. From the edge of the clearing I looked back to it. I was weak as a woman on that day. For another mile or two I stumbled through the snow with a stinging mist across my eyes.

It might be rather sad, rather heroic, to tell of how my heart ached forever after. But here I confine myself to the truth. When I came to the first lower valley, where the snow was gone, the black earth naked or pricked with grasses and early blossoms of wildflowers, when I felt the good warmth of the sun on my face and heard the squirrels talk in the branches above me, I cast away the weight with a gesture.

After all, it might be that this Antoinette, this heiress of the fortunes of Gerardin, would fall deeply and happily in love with *Monsieur* — and live long to enjoy his vast wealth, if she did not long enjoy him. At any rate, it was a thing to be waited for and gazed upon before I went too far into the shadow of self-scorn and despair.

# Chapter
# Twenty-One

# The Return

At the very first town to which I went to buy myself civilized clothes, I was recognized and had to submit to arrest. In two days word came over the wire from all quarters that no charges would be pressed against me by any witnesses and that the state did not care to attack such a hopeless case. So well had my father's agents and his ample purse smoothed the way for me. I took my discharge, received an adequate outfit from the tailor, and started east again.

The darkness was gone from me, except for a sense of distant disaster that was like marking the fall of land on the sea's horizon. I was young enough to enjoy being pointed out, and there had been such wide publishing of my picture, so many tales of my foolish career of brigandage, that I was notorious enough to have tickled the fancy of any rising politician. I was rather prone to eke that journey out as long as possible, because I had a very sharp premonition that, when I reached the Château Limousin, or even the village, my prominence would disappear.

Yet, when I reached the town, there was a buzz as though a prince had arrived. I walked down the street and paused at the old pawnbroker's shop. The sign still hung there, but the windows were a blank. The place was empty. The hand of *Monsieur* had been there before me. I accepted it as a token and went on more gloomily than before, full of thought for that evil little man who had so nearly taken advantage of my innocence less than a year before. In what manner, then, had *Monsieur* attacked him? To whom had he turned when the blow fell? Had he submitted as if to destiny, or had he fought like a desperate cornered rat? Since all mortal men entangle their lives with the lives of others, no matter how slightly, who had felt the loss with him — what children? What wife? What ancient mother or father? What dependent brother? Or was it only someone who cooked his meals and was forced to find other employment when he left the town? As for the little man himself, I had no doubt. *Monsieur* struck heavily, and, after the falling of the blow, there would be nothing left of such a miserable victim.

Perhaps I came next. I could not reason otherwise. Yet I felt that this fragment of a year had matured me wonderfully, giving me strength of which I could not have dreamed at the death of my mother. If it were not strength against my father, it was wisdom to see through him. By the time I had finished computing how much my absence had taught me, I began to feel marvelously reassured. I was in higher spirits when I hired a carriage to drive me to the château.

The coachman had probably heard as much fiction about my adventures as anyone. When we passed others on the road, he could not resist straightening on his seat and tilting his whip over his shoulder a little to call attention to me. When the strangers had passed, he always turned and gave me a joyous grin as if to say: "You see that I call their attention to your excellence."

At twenty-one, anything which seems to make us important can hardly be called ridiculous. I loved that old man for his folly, and, when we reached the château, I gave him such a price and such a tip for his service that he took off his hat and followed me a step or two to bless me.

I took that as a good omen, too — so far was I reduced by the thought of confronting *Monsieur* again. In the rosy dusk of that lovely spring day I stood before the big house, looking at the fine maples that rose over the grave of Hubert Guillaume. The leaves on them were just budding, and through the rosy mist I looked down the avenue that had been cloven through the woods to the waters of the Limousin River, now radiant with the sunset colors. I said to myself that, no matter how pure and how free the air of the western mountains might be, this was the place where I must work out my destiny.

Old Guilbert opened the door and gasped at the sight of me. He wanted to smile and was afraid to — how could he tell how *Monsieur* would greet the returned prodigal? He wanted to give me a greeting but hardly knew an appropriate turn of words. He ended by choking once or twice and taking me to the drawing room. In half a minute *Monsieur* himself was coming. By the faint trembling of the chandelier and the ghostly clinking of some of its pyramid of glass I knew that the heavy step in the hall was his.

He entered with both hands outstretched; he reached me and raised me out of the chair before I had time to rise; he embraced me. How could one forecast the doings of that strange man? I expected him to regard me as a hired servant rather than as a son. Instead, he treated me like a visiting prince.

"Jean, dear Jean! My heart leaps to see you. What? Are you pale and have you lost your tongue? Well, dear lad, if you fear me, I shall not blame you . . . or if you hate me, considering that last scurvy trick of mine. But, Jean, you know that I could not have done what I threatened. You know it now, or you must know it. I was desperate, do you see? It meant so much . . . not for me. No, Jean, but for you . . . your future, the building of this great estate . . . a principality, Jean! Therefore, I did that thing. The trick of a fox. I am ashamed of it . . . you may scorn me if you choose. But tonight let me have the pure joy of welcoming my son home to his house!"

It would have been stupid merely to say: this is not real. Who that has intelligence will sit in the chair and scorn the great actor who makes Lear rave and die before your eyes — because he is really no Lear at all? The art of *Monsieur* carried a lesser soul like myself before it; he swept me away on a wave of enthusiasm as he led me in person to my room. He carried me with him around that room and pointed out everything that had been done to make me welcome. He showed me the white blossoms of potted narcissus that bloomed in the open window. He showed me the gorgeous hangings for the old four-poster bed that I had slept in after infancy. He showed me a closet full of racks of guns.

"You may murder all the wild birds and beasts in the woods, Jean!"

He showed me, last of all, his own special treasure. We paused before it while he explained: "It is my own Rembrandt, Jean. Those who will not admit that it is a Rembrandt are simply afflicted with the jaundice of jealousy. You know that it has always hung in my own room . . . it has been the apple of my eye. When I looked on it last night, when I considered that handsome face under the shadow of that rich cap, the eager eyes of the young painter looked up from his work to his model, the grip of that hand on the top of the drawing board, the other hand poised to make the next line and strike in the whole character of the face he draws . . .

when I saw the sensitive, compressed lips of the youngster, I told myself that it was you. And it should hang in your room, where so many of my thoughts are to be from this day to the end of my life. My happy thoughts, Jean, for all my happiness is to be built upon yours."

Such were the words of *Monsieur*. If I had not tingled with the joy of them, if I had not felt my heart swell, I should have been a poor clay model of a man, not fit to sit in a theater and enjoy the greatest of all arts. I made only the vague effort to criticize him. I had never seen him in such a mood — never dreamed of seeing him in this manner. He was like a happy boy, showing me these treasures that he had lavished upon my homecoming. Yes, I have no doubt that at that moment he *was* a mere boy. He forgot that he was behind footlights, in living and breathing the part. He devoted himself to this fine effort of his imagination.

Perhaps it was more than imagination. Could he have felt some sincere rapture in taking his son back to his home? Ah, well, that I could not tell. I shall never know until this head of mine, powered with the silver of time, has come down to the grave. There let me lie at *Monsieur*'s side, bones beside bones, while our spirits stand face to face in that other world and condemn or save one another by the testimony that only we have the power to give.

I could not know then how much sincerity went with him, but there was enough hope in me to raise my spirits as high as the clouds. To hate *Monsieur* — that was a soul-filling occupation, indeed. If it were possible that I could learn to love him, then earth would surely have been changed to a heaven.

He took me downstairs again. He sent for the butler and bade every domestic in the house be called. He sent for the secretary, an earnest young man named Lafitte, and bade that all the men from the stables, all the gardeners, and all the servants who were enrolled in the huge lists of the château be called in one group. They gathered about the front verandah. My father had the great hanging lamps of the porch lighted and brought me out with him under that white flare of light. I saw the faces tilt up in a pale blur out of the shadows of the twilight and heard an excited murmur run among them.

"Good people," said *Monsieur*, coming forward with his arm around me, "we have come to a happy holiday. There is no work for you tomorrow. There is no work the day after. The cellars of the château are too crowded, my friends. They must be opened to you, and do not fear to call for the old as well as the new. If I see a sober face by the morning, I shall consider that man hates the name of Limousin. And when you drink, remember the name of the dear son who has come back to me!"

They raised a cheer that would have done credit to a regiment of beef-eating Englishmen, and *Monsieur* took me back into the house. There we sat together drinking old, red Burgundy wines that glided through my veins and spread a rich content through my veins. He talked of hunting and of a new Australian wheat that he was planting, of an Irish hunter who winged its way over fences half as high as the moon, of how the deer throve in the preserve, how the trout rose in the brooks, and of how old Guilbert had come running, gasping, stammering, to him with the word: *"Monsieur* Jean! *Monsieur* Jean! He is returned! *Monsieur* Jean in his own flesh, *Monsieur!"*

You must not think that I had forgotten anything, or that I had really forgiven anything, but on this one night I felt that *Monsieur* was gone, in his place was my father.

# Chapter Twenty-Two

# The Guests Arrive

By the morning, two thirds of that vision had dissipated. With the rosy cloud of wine rolled away from my mind, I could find reasons for everything. This enthusiastic welcome was planned and executed in order that I might become a whole-souled, willing collaborator. When poor *Mademoiselle* Gerardin arrived with her aunt, she would be convinced that the rumors that whipped around the countryside were no more than wicked scandals, that there had never been father and son so devoted to one another as we.

That touching little address to the servants was spoken in order that they, with tongues well loosened with wine, might run to the village that night and the next day to tell everyone that they had seen the truth, at last. *Monsieur* did not hate his son, but loved him dearly. If there were any fault between the two, it was the fault of the young man, but never of his good father, who had granted this joyous holiday, so well moistened with fine old wine.

I considered all of these things as any man of sense, no matter how young, must have done. When I went down to breakfast, I paused at the door of my mother's room and tried the knob with a heavy heart. It was locked, and for that I felt a melancholy gratitude to my father. Beyond that gratitude was the bright-faced hope that perhaps a germ of honesty sprang beneath all the skillful acting and inspired it. When I met *Monsieur* in the breakfast room, he was as cheerful as ever. He gave me a quieter yet more sincere welcome, I felt.

Studying him in the morning light, that is the most trying light of all, I wondered over his striking youth. It is seldom that one meets a man with a youthful face and an old body, or a trim, athletic body and features deeply incised by time. My father, despite all his bulk, looked as though he could give a very good account of himself in a ten-mile cross-country run. His skin was as clear as a baby's; his eyes were full, wide, and wonderfully bright, the eyes of a young man, surely. As I grew older, he seemed to step back into youth more and more. I had an absurd, uncomfortable feeling that I must soon be the more age-marked of the two.

He told me, before the breakfast was ended, that Antoinette and her aunt were due to arrive on the afternoon of that very day. I had arrived barely in time to give *Monsieur* my countenance.

By this time I was well reconciled to my part. As *Monsieur* himself had put it, no matter what his crimes had been, it was still absurd to consider that he was not worthy of marrying some obscure girl out of the countryside. As for the disparity in age — she being nineteen and he exactly thirty-two years older — I could not help remarking to myself that, if her spirit remained as young as his for the next ten years, their married life might be happy enough. Before the breakfast ended, I asked him point-blank a question that had tormented me for a long time.

"Was Pierre Reynal acting under your orders and instructions when he followed me west?"

"He brought you a letter," *Monsieur* said frankly. "After that, whatever he did was performed on his own initiative. And on account of that initiative he and I have a long account to settle with one another."

I could not doubt the savage energy with which *Monsieur* spoke. I was consumed with eagerness to ask more questions. He had always hated a cross-examination, and I dared not presume too much upon him.

When the meal ended, he asked me what I wished to do, and, when I told him that I wanted to ride alone through the grounds, I know that he was pleased and relieved. Entertaining his own son was not altogether to the taste of my father. He insisted that I take out one of the Irish hunters; I was to look over all three and select one most to my liking, to be my own.

When I had changed to riding clothes and gone to the stables, McCurdy received me. He was a little Scotch-Irishman whose bandy legs always made him look ridiculous on the back of a horse. He knew the animals by instinct and out of the book. I believe he was the only man on the estate whom my father peculiarly valued; certainly he was the only one who kept a will of his own. It was possible for McCurdy to serve, but never for him to be a servant. He greeted me with a good, hard handgrip and a light in his pale-blue eyes with which he had never favored me in the past. The tales of my wanderings had sunk deeply in the mind of McCurdy — of that I was reasonably sure.

When he heard what I wanted, he had the three hunters saddled and brought to the schooling grounds. Three boys put them over the jumps for my benefit, and I watched them with a critical eye. Any one of them was good enough to suit me. Two were bays, and one a light gray; all were big creatures with a fine, large action and power enough to sport with two hundred and fifty pounds in saddle. I did not wish to appear a fool in the eyes of McCurdy; therefore, I scrutinized them carefully. To save my soul I could not tell which was the best of the lot. Suddenly I turned frankly to McCurdy.

"They look as like as three peas in a pod to me," I said. "Tell me which one I should take."

The grin of McCurdy closed his eyes with satisfaction. "It seems you ain't learned everything there is to know while you were away?" he said. "Well, sir, I've spent thirty years riding and learning horses, but I couldn't find the best of that lot until I'd ridden them myself for a month. It's the gray, *Monsieur* Jean. He is

201

not altogether sound . . . he's broken down a bit in front, and five miles of hard road would cripple him. But he jumps like a bird, and there's nothing but brains in that big, ugly head of his."

I took the gray, and McCurdy put me up on him. While he shortened the stirrups, I could see emotion swelling in him. At last he burst out: "I'm going to ask you a question, *Monsieur* Jean."

"A hundred, if you will."

"One will do for me. Is that true . . . that yarn they tell of how three men came at you through a door . . . and you went through 'em and away?"

"The light was dim in the room," I confessed, "and I took them by surprise. It was not so remarkable as it sounds, McCurdy."

He raised a hand and shook his head to stop these protestations.

"That's all I want to know," he said, stepping back with a broader grin than ever.

I felt that McCurdy was carrying away a tigerish impression of my fighting qualities. I should have been glad to show him the truth, but I knew him well enough to understand that the more I talked, the less he would believe me. When he had made up his Scotch-Irish mind, nothing but death could change him. So I rode off through the woods, never dreaming how much the devotion of McCurdy was to mean to me before many weeks were ended.

How many acres belonged to *Monsieur* I do not, to this day, know accurately, but I rode hard until noon brought me back to the Château Limousin, weaving along forest paths, sweeping along the broadbacked hills, or striding big over the broad valley lands. Never once in that ride was I off the estate. Only twice did I skirt the huge stone wall that marked the boundary. It was as happy a ride as I had ever taken, and I came back to fill the ears of McCurdy with the praises of my new horse and thank him for the selection. Then I went to the château to prepare for the ordeal of the afternoon.

The old clock in the hall was striking four with a deep voice when I heard the wheels of a carriage crunching the gravel of the driveway. Then, through my open door, I could hear the faint tinkle of feminine voices mixed with the heavy tone of my father. An instant later someone came to tell me that they had arrived and I could properly go down to them. I mustered my facial expression on the way and prepared my picture of them. Marcia Gerardin would be an old maid of an indeterminate age between forty and fifty — which one could take to mean fifty, at least. She was probably sour, thin, polite, reserved. As for her niece, I had partly gathered from what *Monsieur* had said — although he had never seen her — that she was an undistinguished little country girl. By this time she probably was sitting in a frightened hush, contemplating the Château Limousin and the stern and famous master of the house. With such people as these I felt that it would not be too difficult to play my part of affability toward my father. My only wish was that the dirty business might be ended as soon as possible, and that I could get away to that European life that *Monsieur* had promised me.

In a word, I had been bought, body and soul. Although at that time my father had drawn me forward step by step and surrounded me with his pleasantest atmosphere, yet, even then, I knew in my heart the full vileness of the thing I was about to do.

So it was that I came in to them, to find all of my preconceptions beaten to the ground. My first thought was that *Mon-*

*sieur* had again deceived me; my second thought was that he himself probably had not known.

Before I reached the door of the room, I heard a woman — it was *Mademoiselle* Marcia, because it could not be a girl — saying in English without a trace of French accent in it: "But that frightful brute stretched out his long neck and took the reins out of my hands. He took me through the forest like a devil with wings, and, when the sunlight smashed in my face on the far side of the trees, I was too bewildered to take my bearings at once. Then I saw the hounds not fifty strides away, with the fox getting weary . . . just in front of them, its tail down . . . and not another rider in sight! That, *Monsieur* Limousin, was the only time I was in at the kill, and that was how I got there. As a rule, the third or fourth fence finishes me. I was built for rolling off a saddle, not for sitting in one. If God had not furnished these bones of mine with such a comfortable padding, they would all have been broken long ago."

With this she broke into a great laughter, in the midst of which I came through the door of the room and had my first view of her.

# Chapter Twenty-Three

# Mademoiselle Marcia

She was made to fit her voice, this Marcia Gerardin. That is to say, her voice was clearly feminine enough, but it was strong, big, dominating. It was such a voice, I should say, as makes others raise their own speaking tones until a room is full of clamor. She stood by the window with one hand resting jauntily on her hip — a big, strong hand. She had wide shoulders that would have done credit to most men, and a broad, brown, outdoors face. In spite of her masculine way and her assurance, in spite of the bigness of her voice, I knew at once that she was refined. She came forward a little to meet me. *Monsieur* was murmuring an introduction, but she drowned his voice at once.

"Come here to the window, young man," she said. "I've grown as near-sighted as a bat, and I want to see every bit of you. Ah, Jean Limousin, how could one guess that you are such a tiger under the skin? Because it seems to me that you are simply a very nice, good-looking boy. Does it not seem so, *Monsieur* Limousin? Does it not seem so, Antoinette? Yet how much he has made us talk about him for a year."

As a rule, a youngster hates the person who drags him into view, robbed of his dignity, like a prize dog. She was so entirely unaffected and so good-natured that I could smile back at her without the slightest malice. Then I went over to Antoinette Gerardin.

If I say that the reality of *Mademoiselle* Marcia reversed all my preconceptions of what she must be, Antoinette was still more a surprise to me. She was a beauty of Southland type, with an Italian skin, clear but olive-stained, and very large, very black eyes. I should say in passing from *Mademoiselle* Gerardin to *Mademoiselle* Antoinette, I was passing from boisterous wind and blazing sun into shadow. She spoke quietly to me, with a faint smile at her aunt — as though to intimate that she enjoyed the enthusiasm of Aunt Marcia even while she was amused by it. That smile told me that they were excellent good friends, that there was a brain behind the dark eyes of *Monsieur*'s future wife, that for all the noise and the stir of Aunt Marcia, Antoinette was doubtless the stronger soul. What else I gathered from that first instant with Antoinette I cannot put into words, unless it is possible to render in adequate terms all that passes through the mind, say, when the first softness of spring breathes out of the ground, or when the first threads of color run through the autumn woods.

I felt like entering at once into a hearty conversation with Aunt Marcia. I wanted to sit back and watch Antoinette. But there was little opportunity to sit in observant quiet when Marcia Gerardin was near. She observed in her own way that the château was a fine house and worth seeing, but: "I wait for dark days to look at interiors, and now the sunshine is going to waste in bucketfuls!"

In half an hour she had tumbled herself into riding clothes and came striding out to the horses with us, while Antoinette stepped at her side like a slim princess. I had never had such an occasion to use eyes and ears. The Gerardins were enough to watch, and different enough, also, but before that ride ended I think it was *Monsieur* who had the greater part of my attention.

He had lost most of the high spirits that had filled him during the past two days. Instead, he was grown rather moodily silent. By that I knew that he was profoundly excited. Before we had returned I had guessed the reason — Antoinette. As he had confessed to me, he had never seen her before, not so much as her picture. Therefore, she had been as much of a shock to him as to me. It was more than a light pleasure to him; he was seriously and deeply moved — how much moved I, at the time, did not guess.

When I came down the stairs the next morning for breakfast, I found that the picture of *Monsieur*'s first wife, the only real passion in all his existence, was gone from above the great fireplace of the library.

The fall of a city, the destruction of an army could not have meant so much in my eyes. From that moment I knew that *Monsieur* loved the girl as he had never loved before. All my objections to the part I was to play should have been removed instantly, but, strange to say, they were not. From the time of that ride, and particularly from the moment I missed the big oil painting in the library, I felt a rooted aversion for this match that had never existed in me before. As I watched *Monsieur,* day after day, courting Antoinette as seriously, as gravely, as any youth carried away by a first romantic impulse, my anger and my horror grew.

Marcia Gerardin was, naturally, much with me during those days. I came to love her frankness and her bubbling talk. She could not have been more candid with me if I had been her brother. The first real explosion of her mind came as we sat under a tree beside the tennis courts, watching Antoinette play with *Monsieur* — she flashing here and there, flushed and filled with the joy of the game, *Monsieur* gliding easily on the other side of the net.

"Look," muttered *Mademoiselle* Marcia beneath her breath. "I think that *Monsieur* is allowing Antoinette to win."

"Perhaps," I replied.

"Ah, but you know his game . . . and he can stroke more severely than this, can he not?"

Remembering some of the mighty duels he had had with Pierre Reynal, how the ball had disappeared in the bright sunlight, dissolved with speed as they hammered it back and forth, I could not help smiling.

"Well, I could tell," my companion went on. "I used to play the game very fairly, but the time came when I had to choose between butter and tennis, and, of course, like a sensible person, I chose butter. I know enough to see that he is working inside his strength, and that is not like him . . . that is very unlike him."

"Is it so unusual?" I asked her.

"Tush!" she exclaimed. "You know as well as I do that he is a man who always wins if he can. He is always the victor . . . and there goes a set to Antoinette, as I live."

As they changed courts, we heard the girl say: "You are not doing your best, *Monsieur* Limousin. You are not using your full strength."

"I am afraid to," said *Monsieur*. "I am too inaccurate at this season of the year."

They began again, and suddenly *Monsieur* changed his style. The softness of his stroking disappeared; the ball began to wink out of view in mid-air with the terrible power of his driving. Antoinette, gasping with excitement, raced back and forth, fighting her best, but *Monsieur*'s own errors, so it seemed, were defeating him. That day he was inspired with the racquet. I have never seen better play. His cannon-shot volleys over passed the back line by scant inches; his terrible passing shots skimmed across the sidelines by as narrow a margin. He was playing most wonderfully, his great breast heaving with the violence of the work. Still his errors were giving her points, although she could not get a racquet on the ball, except to pop it fruitlessly high in the air.

Marcia Gerardin studied this display with her chin on her clenched fist and her fat elbow on her knee. "Ah . . . ah . . . ah!" she exclaimed. "I am right! I thought it was to be a mere commercial alliance . . . a distinguished and successful business contract . . . but, by heaven, I think it is to be a love match. Do you not, *Monsieur* Jean?"

She had that bad habit of making her questions as point-blank as her own remarks. A thousand times I have had to bite my lip before I could answer her. This time she did not allow me sufficient time to make a response. She said, smiling at me: "You would never make a very successful deceiver, *Monsieur* Jean. It takes you too long to invent . . . whereas *Monsieur* . . . why, he has composed an entire story before the question is out of one's mouth. You should do well to study him, Jean."

The reply came from me involuntarily.

"How can one study a lightning flash?" Then I bit my lip again.

"There, there, there," she said, chuckling. "I have surprised one precious morsel of truth from you. However, I shall not press the point. Only, as I asked you before, do you not think that it will be a love match . . . at least on the side of *Monsieur?*"

"I have no doubt," I responded politely, "and therefore on both sides."

"Which means," she asked, "that if *Monsieur* decided to love Antoinette as well as her lands, it will follow as a matter of course that she must love him?"

It was the sort of ground that I most disliked to walk upon, but her eyes were fixed so steadily upon me that I had to make some sort of a reply.

"I cannot imagine," I said carefully, "that anyone could resist *Monsieur* . . . that is, when he is inclined to be amiable."

"And when he is otherwise inclined? However, although you may know *Monsieur* very well, I confess that I do not know Antoinette. Sometimes, when I see how far we have gone in this affair, I don't know how she could draw out of it. But then, again, I cannot tell . . . I cannot tell."

I could not help saying coldly: "It would

be impossible, of course, for *Mademoiselle* Gerardin to enter an alliance for the sake of . . . mere social consideration."

My strange companion broke into laughter. "Jean, Jean!" she cried. "What a sweet, romantic child you are. Are you frightfully angry with me now?"

"By no means."

"Oh, but you are! Your nice blue eyes are filled with fire, your brown face is covered with scarlet, and you have set your square jaw. You are exceedingly angry, Jean."

I tried to laugh; it was a foolish attempt. "One hopes to leave one's childhood . . . after a certain time," I said with all the dignity that I could present for the occasion.

"Does one hope so?" she asked, hugging her knees from the excess of amusement. "This one, however, does not hope so. You see, Jean, I am still too young to marry. Men cannot abide my foolish ways . . . not even young men."

Here she began to laugh until the tears filled her eyes and ran down her quivering cheeks. After which she borrowed my handkerchief to dry her face. I cannot tell why I did not hate that woman, but I did not. There was something about her that never failed to find a tickling chord in my heart. I was chuckling in turn before she had finished her laughter.

"Dear Jean!" she cried. "How I love you, because you can laugh at yourself. However, let me tell you that it would *not* be impossible for *Mademoiselle* Gerardin . . . why don't you call her Antoinette and have done with it? . . . to enter an alliance for mere social considerations."

This repetition of my words made her pass off into another breeze of laughter. I waited patiently, smiling at her. In fact, I had come to be wonderfully fond of her.

"Social considerations," she went on, "like this château and the sweep of lands around it are considerations that might make a duchess chuck her title into a handbag and take the next steamer for Quebec. However, I confess again that I cannot tell about Antoinette. I think I have brought her so far that she will sign a treaty. But whether I can make her come to the altar . . . no, that I certainly cannot tell."

You cannot imagine a woman in her position talking in this open fashion to the son of *Monsieur,* and at such a time. Neither can I imagine it, other than from the throat of Marcia Gerardin.

"Jean," she said, "I think that there is one thing which would convince Antoinette instantly."

"Convince her of what?" I asked.

"That marriage with *Monsieur* is a wise measure."

"And that?"

"If she could make sure from your own lips that the rumor which went through the country was not true, that *Monsieur* did *not* cause the death of your mother and your flight from the château."

# Chapter Twenty-Four

# Triumph

I repeated these startling words of *Mademoiselle* Gerardin two or three times, getting the meaning into my brain. Then she said: "I had not meant to cut you so really deep, Jean."

"It is nothing," I assured her.

"This is the Limousin in you . . . even in you," she said. "Well, do not answer me."

"Are you not already answered?" I countered. "Am I not here at the château? Are not my father and I upon the best relations?"

"Exactly!" cried this odd woman. "I have pointed that out a thousand times to Antoinette. But she is troubled with a sort of extra sense, Jean, which comes between her and what she sees and hears. On this question, I tell you, she is a queer girl, and,

217

when I try to overwhelm all of her objections, what do you think she says?"

"I cannot tell. What is it that she says?"

"That there is something wrong with the château. Why, one would think it was full of ghosts, to hear her. Do you wonder that I think her a queer girl?"

"I do not, *mademoiselle*," I said.

After that I tried to escape from her, for I dreaded more of these same questions as I dreaded a trial by fire. Marcia Gerardin had been educated in England, which I presume was the reason of her fondness for that language and the cause of her blunt, open manner of speech. I liked her, I think, more than ever after this conversation. Also, I dreaded her more. Above all, I feared lest she should carry her suggestion to *Monsieur*. What would happen if he put pressure upon me to give Antoinette Gerardin any direct assurance that all was well and never had been otherwise between my father and me? I thought that there was something in me that would keep me bowing to his will in this matter. How little I knew his strength and my weakness.

The very next day put me, as I considered, past this danger. I had gone down to the edge of the river and launched a canoe

in the late afternoon — the most en-
chanting time upon the water — when I
heard the voice of *Monsieur* calling for me
through the trees. His call always made me
wish to run away. I obeyed that impulse
now to the extent of shooting the canoe a
few strokes down the lee of the riverbank. I
saw then that this was folly, so I backed
water and answered him. He came crashing through the shrubbery in another moment. That was his way of going through
underbrush, unless he were stalking; otherwise, he chose to smash through by sheer
strength, as he did now, laughing at the
sharp branch points and the whip-like
limbs. He came into my view with his hat
knocked to one side, his blue flannel coat
covered with leaves and dust, and a jagged
rent in his white trousers.

"It is done, Jean!" he shouted, waving
down to me.

"What is that, *Monsieur?*" I asked him,
guessing very well but seeing that he
wished to talk and explain.

"Have you an extra paddle there?"

"I have, *Monsieur.*"

He sprang instantly into the canoe with
the perfect balance of any sailor, and
squatting in the prow — well back so that
he would not dip the nose of the little craft

too deeply — he started us off into the river with powerful thrusts of his paddle.

"I must be on the water more, Jean!" he called over his shoulder. "This is glorious . . . besides, she tells me that she loves canoeing. Why have you not taken her out, Jean? Is there no spirit in you, lad?"

"*Monsieur,* you have monopolized her shamefully. I have had no opportunity."

His great laughter went booming and reëchoing away out across the water. "Have I not? Have I not?"

He had been shooting us through the water at a tremendous pace by his mighty paddle work. Now, by an evolution that nearly capsized the frail boat, he whirled himself around and sat facing me, the shining paddle across his knees.

"Could any youth," my father asked, "have made a stronger dead set at a girl than I have made at her?"

No young man, of course, could have spoken in this fashion of an affair of his heart, but *Monsieur* knew no shame — no more than a king of other days, whose vices were splendid because they were a king's.

"You have surrounded her with attention," I admitted, wondering if, in my middle age, I could ever reach such a stage of simplicity. He was like a very young boy, full of an exploit — like a barbarian ready to boast. I kept up a steady pace with my paddle, glad of the work that gave employment to my hands and permitted me to shift my glance from his blazing eyes to pick our course.

"Ah," said *Monsieur,* "what a difficult game it has been." He sighed and laughed at the same time. "Because," he went on, "I could not put it on the basis of love . . . merely as a sensible alliance. That was how I had to present the case to her. Without the help of Marcia I should have been lost. May she inherit a crown in heaven for her good work. But the double pressure has been too much. How do you think, Jean, that I finally approached this Venus, this wise and lovely girl?"

My face grew hot. I hoped that he would attribute it to the work of paddling, and, therefore, I labored more arduously than ever.

"I shall tell you. We had come in from the tennis courts. I had taken the racquet from her hand. I had turned over a dozen situations in my mind, trying to select the proper one, but gradually coming to know that the least touch of romance or of passion would be repulsive to her. So I said, as

221

I wiped my forehead with my handkerchief
. . . ha! ha! ha! . . . Jean, was not that a
moment for a proposal?"

"It was a strange moment," I agreed,
choking with distaste and wishing with all
my heart that I did not have to listen to his
next words.

"I said to her . . . 'My dear Antoinette,
you have beaten me so outrageously today
that I should like to keep you with me a
long time until I get my revenge. I should
like to keep you indefinitely, Antoinette.'
What do you say to that, Jean? It was not
bad, I imagine. It was worthy of being put
into a book, I presume. Sometimes, Jean,
when I consider myself, I wonder that I do
not sit down and write out some of the
things that are in my mind. But it would be
strong meat, intended only for strong men
. . . and the world is full of babies. Babies!"

"Perhaps that is true," I replied.

"Do you know, Jean, that, although her
eye is so softly feminine, yet it is the only
one I have ever encountered . . . except
that devil Reynal's . . . that could look
fairly into mine without drooping or
growing unsteady? When I said that to her,
she looked up to me in her quiet way.

" 'I suppose that I understand you?' she
said.

" 'You do,' I told her.

" 'Shall I be honest?' she asked me.

"Then I trembled. I, François Limousin, trembled before this child. 'By all means be honest,' I said.

" 'I admire you, *Monsieur*,' she stated, 'and I think I might easily be afraid of you. But, also, I do not think that I could ever love you.'

"My heart stood still. My heart, Jean, not the heart of some mooncalf boy.

" 'Is love, then,' I asked, 'the only good motive for action in our lives?'

" 'I think not,' she responded.

"I breathed again. She went on . . . 'I believe that my father and my mother married for the purest love. But they had an unhappy home. Love makes a tyrant of a man and of a woman. I should be afraid of myself and of the future if I were in danger of falling in love.'

" 'Antoinette,' I could not help breaking in on her, 'you speak like a woman of mature sense.'

" 'Thank you,' she said. 'And thank you, too, for the offer you make me. I have tried to look clearly at this thing, *Monsieur*. I have talked it over very carefully with my Aunt Marcia. And I hope it is not wrong for me to say that, since you wish me, I shall become your wife, *Monsieur.*'

"Jean, is not that enough to make you stop your paddling and wonder?"

Glad that I had been able to cover my emotion so well that he did not suspect me, I said: "I congratulate you, *Monsieur.*"

"But throw your paddle in the air . . . shout . . . strike your hands together! It is no ordinary woman. It is she! It is this strange and beautiful Antoinette who is to be my wife!"

"I trust that you will have nothing but happiness, *Monsieur.*"

"So cold?" he stated, puzzled. "Ah, well, I wonder at you, Jean. You are too young, I suppose, to care for her. You wish a more dainty dish. You will have some delicate blonde with baby-blue eyes and a soft mouth that even smiling spoils, a hand like crumpling rose petals, a voice like tinkling music, and a brain and soul not yet fit to leave the cradle. That will be the love and the wife for you, Jean. But if I could strip before your eyes the strong heart and the noble soul of this girl, you would fall upon your knees and worship her."

This was spoken by *Monsieur,* not by some village lover. I did not need his voice to teach me what I had guessed already. Yet, after all, she was to be his wife.

"I live in heaven, therefore," *Monsieur* continued. "I live in heaven, but the sword is suspended over my head by a strand of most delicate silk. The last touch lets it fall, and my happiness dies. She is full of doubts. She is full of suspicions. I think it is because she half fears me, because she has glimpses of the devil in me, that she is willing to marry me. Danger is attractive. It appeals to an imp of the perverse in us. Besides, she loves strength. When I smashed the tennis ball at her so hard that it almost tore the racquet out of her hand, she laughed. And yet not masculine, Jean. All woman. A fragrance. An intoxication. And by a single touch I lose her. Turn back to the shore, Jean . . . quickly, quickly! I must see her again."

He picked up his paddle again, turned into his place, and gave to the boat the power of a driving motor. He kept on until the prow was wedged deeply in the sand, and then he leaped on shore with a violence that almost upset the little craft. Halfway up the bank, however, he paused again.

"No," he said, speaking his thoughts aloud, "no, no! I must not be too impulsive. She has seen enough of me for the moment. She has seen quite enough. If she remains too much near the secret, she will guess it. Come ashore, Jean."

He dragged up the boat with me in it as lightly as though it had been a feather. When I stood at his side, he put a hand on my shoulder.

"I have another thought which is better," *Monsieur* then announced. "I have persuaded her to remain at the château until the marriage. Now she is in my hand, and, to keep her from slipping out, I shall leave her much with you. It grows upon me. Do you see, Jean, that, while she is with you, she will read me by what she finds in you. If she finds in you a gentle and sensitive soul, she will remember that you are my son, and, therefore, you will be a glass through which she looks and thinks she discovers certain new and delightful things in me."

He began to laugh again. With his arm through mine he dragged me up the slope. My heart was too full to deny him.

# Chapter Twenty-Five

# A Groan in the Night

We followed toward the house the same path along which my mother and I had walked almost a year before. *Monsieur* was chattering gaily every step of the way, and, when we came from the edge of the forest into the view of the château, he paused to say: "We'll make a garden there, Jean. Do you see? It will keep her amused. I must suggest it to her tonight. Then she can plan it during the next two weeks. Nothing like work to keep people out of mischief."

"And the marriage, *Monsieur?*"

"In a fortnight."

"So soon?"

"Soon? It is fourteen eternities away . . . fourteen endless days during any moment of which she may slip out of my hand. But I lean on you, Jean. I trust you."

"You are wrong," I said. "Suppose that she were to turn my head, as she has turned yours?"

He quickly laughed that thought to scorn. "You would never dare," he said. "Besides, she is not the proper type for you. Ah, I know your mind too well."

I endured this conversation in silence. It was the first time he had shown his direct scorn of me since I had returned to the château, and, therefore, the sting of it was more bitter. However, having accepted my work, it was not for me to make difficulties over small things.

In the library, before dinner, the announcement was made very quietly. Marcia Gerardin embraced her niece. I shook hands with Antoinette and *Monsieur,* congratulating them. Then we had a glass of wine together. That was all there was to it. I could not help fixing my eyes upon the girl to see if she did not change color. She showed not the least emotion, so far as I could make out. Her poise was as perfect as though she had merely heard *Monsieur* read a piece out of a paper.

So she was sold.

I did not realize that I had cared so

much. To think of all this beauty, this gentleness, this wisdom, passing like a purchased thing into the hands of *Monsieur* so sickened me that I left them early and went up to my room. I believe that I sensed something as I came through the doorway. As I turned up the flame in the throat of the chimney, a little shudder of cold went through me. I knew that it was Pierre Reynal before I whirled around and found him seated in the corner of the room.

He stood up and bowed to me with a good deal of dignity. As usual, I did not know how to deal with him.

"I have not expected you, Reynal," I said at length. "And it's only proper to warn you that you are not wise to come here. Perhaps you do not know that *Monsieur* has conceived a terrible dislike for you. It is really not safe for you to be here, Reynal."

"I think that I have no business with *Monsieur*," he responded. "I hope that I have not," he added with a solemnity that I was to remember afterward.

"You have come to talk with me only?"

"That is it."

I glanced at him more deeply. He was very badly dressed, in a leather, hunting jacket, with moccasins on his feet, and trousers that were shabby wrecks. Even his hat was battered out of shape. A new thought came to me.

"It is money, then, Pierre," I suggested more gently than I thought I could have spoken to him. The long months of companionship in the mountains had taken away some of my horror of the monster. "You have had bad luck, and so you have remembered me. Is that it?"

Here he leaned a little forward in his chair and stared at me. "And if I did?" he asked in his harsh voice. "And if I did, *Monsieur* Jean?"

"I am glad to say that I am in a position to be of help to you. My father is generous to his servants."

"I believe that you would do it," said Pierre Reynal with a good deal of emotion. "I believe that you would turn your purse into my hand. God bless you for that, *Monsieur* Jean. It makes me hope, for the moment, that you have forgiven me."

"You are excited, Reynal," I said more coldly. "You speak as if you were ill. Is there anything wrong with you?"

"Nothing," he stated, recovering his self-possession at once. "There is nothing wrong with me."

"Then will you tell me your errand here?"

"I have waited, *Monsieur* Jean, until you had a chance to see the château and the people in it again. You have had time enough for that?"

"Certainly. What point is there to that?"

"A great point. You will have seen by this time that it is ruin for you to remain."

I was more angered than surprised. No matter how clearly I saw the same thing, it was a poisonous thing to hear another man reproach me.

"What under heaven do you wish, Reynal?" I asked him.

"Under heaven," he said with the same gravity that he had used before, "I hope to persuade you to leave the château."

"You speak like a priest, Reynal. Have you not studied for the clergy?"

He staggered me by replying calmly: "I have, *Monsieur* Jean."

"You!" I cried, remembering in a hot flood all the things that I held against him — and the list was long. Then I added with a sneer: "What induced you to give up the good work, Pierre?"

"A woman, *Monsieur*," he replied.

I never was sure when he was mocking me and when he was serious, because the frightful leer into which his face was perpetually drawn added a touch of irony to

231

everything that he spoke. Yet I had never known him actually to be guilty of a jest. I turned this last sentence of his back and forth in my mind, guessing at many new things in my old enemy. For a moment I almost believed him, almost pitied him. Then I said: "Whatever I do, I think it will not be because you have influenced me. That is my hope, at least. Since you are so curious about it, I will confess that I do not intend to remain long at the château. I shall be here no longer than the day of the marriage."

"So!" cried Reynal, with his eye lighting. "You are to be married! To that beautiful dark-haired girl, is it not?"

"No, not I. My father."

He started convulsively out of his chair. "What is that?"

"You seem to wonder at it. Is it the difference in their years? But the heart of *Monsieur* is young."

"*Monsieur* Limousin," Reynal murmured like a bewildered man spelling out a strange thing in order to make sure of it, "is to marry again?"

"I have said it."

"It is not possible!"

"In fact, it is, though. They are to be married within two weeks. After that I leave the château."

"God will not permit it," Reynal declared in such a voice that I was amazed again. "He will not allow more blood to be shed. God will not permit it, *Monsieur* Jean."

It filled me with sorrow and fury. I stated: "You have said enough, Reynal, and more than enough."

"Perhaps that is true," muttered Reynal. "As for the other things which I have to say to you . . . they may wait. But this . . . but this. . . ." He went to the door. "*Adieu, Monsieur* Jean. I shall see you again."

I made him no answer, and he went out, closing the door softly behind him. When he was gone, however, I felt that I must ask him a hundred questions more because, from what he had said, I had begun to guess at a thousand things, pointing I knew not toward what.

When I snatched open my door, however, he was not there. I thought, at first, that he might have gone to the next story above, in order to get to the back of the house and so down again by a little winding staircase that was rarely used. I was sure that, after my warning to him, he would not trust to the chance that one of the servants might see him.

When I reached the third story, there was no sight of him. I had followed so rapidly that I was sure he could not have reached the end of the long upper hall. I came down again, half bewildered, wondering if that strange man might not have ventured through the main section of the house in spite of danger. I passed my own room, and at the next turn of the hall I stopped abruptly. There stood the tall shadow of Pierre Reynal, stooped before the locked door of my mother's room. While I watched, I saw his hand slowly and reverently trace a cross upon head and breast.

Not waiting to see any more, I stole back to my own room. My father had never favored the teaching of religious lessons in the château. Yet when I saw such a man as Pierre Reynal in prayer before the door of my mother's room, I was wonderfully touched. Indeed, he had done her enough harm to pray for the peace of her soul and for her forgiveness.

I lay down on the couch before the open fire in my room — for this spring night was sharp with cold — and I fell deeply asleep, not awakening until it was past midnight. By that time the fire had burned down to dull embers — a mere streaking of rust in the ashes of the hearth — and the chill of the air had awakened me thoroughly. I decided to read myself asleep. Wrapping myself in a dressing gown, I turned up the light and selected a book. Suddenly I heard from what I thought was the direction of *Monsieur*'s room a sound like a stifled groan and then a stamping of feet.

# Chapter Twenty-Six

# A Midnight Battle

I went for that room by the shortest route —
that is to say, through my door onto the balcony, and down the balcony to the window
of *Monsieur*'s room. He had been reading in
bed. The lamp stood on the bedside table,
but the book lay crushed, face down upon
the floor. The bedclothes had been stripped
wildly off the mattress and now pointed, like
a great white hand, toward a corner where
two men struggled.

Pushing the French door in with my
shoulder, I lurched into the chamber. *Monsieur*, in his pajamas, his activity masked by
an entangling dressing gown, lay on his
back, beating and tearing at the face of a
rudely dressed man who, with head down,
had sunk his fingers in the throat of my father. I was too horrified to cry out; I

merely threw myself on that murderous assailant.

It was like attacking the power of a writhing python. I was thrust back in an instant. A powerful blow in the face tumbled me, half senseless, upon the floor. As I struggled again to my feet, I saw Pierre Reynal leap from the body of *Monsieur* and race on his moccasined feet to the balcony. I let him go.

My father lay with purpled face, his eyes thrusting out from his head. By the time I had brought water, he was already sitting up, gasping, his head bent far back on his shoulders as he drank in the life-giving air. I helped him to his feet, and the trembling, helpless bulk, which I supported, taught me how far spent he really had been. As he sank into the chair, his head falling feebly against the cushion, I saw the reddened base of his throat where the thumbs of Reynal had been biting to cut off the air. Another ten seconds, or five, perhaps, and there would have been an end. I found a brandy bottle and brought him a glass of it. He drank with a hand trembling so much that half the contents spilled out along the front of his pajama coat.

What I chiefly marveled at was that any man could have mastered the Herculean strength of *Monsieur,* as Reynal had done. I looked to see some bruise or sign of a blow upon the head, but there was none. By the naked power of his hands, Reynal had done this thing and come within a breath of taking the life of the ruler of Limousin.

Someone began to tap at the door with an increasing insistence and loudness.

"Answer!" gasped out my father. "Remember. There is nothing wrong."

I gaped at him, and he repeated: "There is nothing wrong."

From the inside of the door I asked who was there, and the uneven voice of the new secretary, Lafitte, answered from the hall: "In my room above this, I heard strange noises which I thought came from your room."

"This is Jean Limousin," I said. "There is nothing wrong."

There was a slight pause. I thought that he had turned away, when he asked in a more excited manner than before: "I beg ten thousand pardons, *Monsieur* Jean, but may I not hear the voice of *Monsieur* himself?"

It was a very good token of the resolute honesty and courage of Lafitte that he should have stuck to his post in this manner, but the mere asking of that question made the hair prickle upon my head with the frightful insinuations that it made.

My father, however, had by this time so far recovered his breath that he was able to call out, in a hoarse, strained voice: "There is no trouble, Lafitte. Run along to bed, my good fellow. There is nothing wrong."

I heard Lafitte clear his throat in an undecided fashion as though this answer did not at all satisfy him — and well it might not. If he had heard what I had heard, plus the sound of the French door to the balcony broken in by my shoulder, and the turmoil of my attack upon Reynal added to the rest, he had, indeed, heard enough to alarm him thoroughly. At length his footsteps went along the hall, and I turned back to my father.

He had recuperated wonderfully, and, although his face was still swollen and crimson, he had lighted a cigarette and was smoking it, but with a shaking hand on which there was a drop of crimson. He seemed to be ashamed of the situation in which I had found him. Already he had thrown the bedding back on the bed, had reordered his dressing gown, and was combing his thick, short beard into a better trim. He greeted me with: "Well,

Jean, I was about to tear the scoundrel's head from his shoulders when you broke in and let him escape in the mix-up."

"Really?" I asked, with an irresistible impulse to smile at this easy invention. "I am sorry that I came in on you, then."

At this he laughed in a broken, wheezing voice, caressing his bruised throat carefully. "No, Jean, no. It will not do, I see. No, I must confess that I was nearly a dead man. The devil is a practiced wrestler . . . a practiced assassin, I meant to say. He took that stranglehold before I fairly knew that he intended to attack me. But if I have a chance at him again, I promise you that I shall break the villain in two."

You must consider that this was a man past fifty years in age, and yet his first impulse, after being saved from the most imminent and frightful danger, was to escape the odium of having needed a rescuer. I made things as easy for him as I could.

"He has taught me some of his wrestling tricks," I said. "He has an iron grip, *Monsieur.*"

"One would not have guessed that he had taught you much," said *Monsieur,* "to judge by the ease with which he plucked you away and flattened you on the floor."

"He could master me in an instant," I

confessed, "or almost any other man, I think."

"That is an admission for a young skull cracker and gun handler with your reputation. But I think that you are right, and I need not be so shamed."

"But, *Monsieur*," I could not help breaking in, "is he to escape in this fashion?"

From what Reynal had said to me when he was in my room on that same night, I knew now that he had planned some such an attack as this even at that time. But, if he intended to kill, why did he not fall back upon his unrivaled skill with deadly weapons?

*Monsieur* answered: "If I wanted a pursuit of him, I should have given an alarm long before this. No, that is not to the point. I do not care to have him handled by the law. Let us use our own ways and our own laws upon this assassin, Jean."

"As you please, sir."

"Another thing, Jean . . . do not let a word of this come out tomorrow. And Lafitte . . . I must warn him . . . no, you must give him the warning for me. Do you understand?"

"I do."

"Go to him at once, then. He is an unimaginative man. He may take this too seriously. And there has been a great deal of talk about strange occurrences in the Château Limousin. Go to him now, Jean. But first, I thank you, lad, for your quick, bold way of going at Reynal. I may say that I owe my life to you . . . as you owe yours to me. And so we part equal, do we not?"

He could not for an instant admit an obligation to another man. It was the worst of torments for him to do so. For my part, I would have given a very great deal to know how Reynal had entered the room. The French door had been locked, and the door to the hall was locked, also. It must have been, so far as I could see, that *Monsieur* himself had admitted Reynal, and then, after some talk with him, there had been a sudden and a tigerish attack.

What had passed between them, then, before the struggle commenced? But, if my father did not choose to speak of it, there was nothing I could do to gain an understanding of the encounter. Only this much was very clear — the old alliance that I had so long suspected between Reynal and *Monsieur* could never have existed, except in my imagination. That made the events that ended in the death of my mother more mysterious than ever.

I thought of these things as I hastened up to the door of Lafitte's room. When he opened it to me, he was already fully dressed, and his revolver lay on the table in the center of the chamber.

"It was a mere nothing," I announced to Lafitte. "I was speaking with *Monsieur* in his room, and, as I left him, I tripped on a rolled-up corner of the rug and upset the table with the books on it. You understand, *Monsieur* Lafitte?"

He looked at me straight in the eye after the fashion of one who tries to read the truth that may exist behind a lie. "Very well, *Monsieur* Jean," he said. "It is not my place to doubt what you say to me."

"However," I went on, striving to improve my story with a little more elaboration, "*Monsieur* is much impressed by the speed with which you came down to his room. If there *had* been a danger . . . you understand that *Monsieur* conveys you his thanks!"

Lafitte did not smile. He merely bowed in acknowledgment. "*Monsieur* is very kind," he declared coldly. "What seemed remarkable to me was the length of time during which the books continued . . . er . . . to fall from the table, *Monsieur* Jean."

This was a remark so pointed that I

could not very well find an immediate answer to it. Moreover, from the hostile manner of Lafitte, I could not help deducing that he believed there had actually been a physical encounter between my father and me. However, considering the strange tales that had circulated through the countryside after the death of my mother, this attitude was not so extraordinary.

It left me nothing to do but turn my back on the matter with a very confused face and go back to the apartment of *Monsieur*. I had to tell him what the rumor would be, if Lafitte or anyone else in the house started one.

I found *Monsieur* bathing his throat with cold water and examining the bruises in the mirror with many oaths. He listened blandly while I explained that, if the tale were told, it would be a frightful story of an unnatural midnight battle between *Monsieur* and his son. He was as much agitated as I, but for different reasons.

"And if this story should come to the ears of Antoinette," he lamented, "ah, I shall most assuredly find a way of capturing Pierre Reynal and tearing him limb from limb. Go back to your room, however. Sleep well. Tomorrow you must be cheerful and pleasant for my sake, Jean."

# Chapter Twenty-Seven

# The Fairy Princess

The very next day I was forced to take up the burden of *Monsieur* with beautiful Antoinette Gerardin. My father was hoarse, and I believe that he had a frightful headache from the struggle of the night before. At any rate, he pleaded the necessity of a business trip and left the two ladies in my hands. It could not have been done at a more unwelcome time. My own head was buzzing with imaginations that bore upon Pierre Reynal and his odd adventure. Moreover, my amiable tormentor, Aunt Marcia, insisted that they take advantage of me.

"Because, Antoinette," she said, "you will have enough to do with middle-aged people after a few days, and you must not miss a chance to enjoy a youngster like Jean Limousin. As for me, my need is just as great because I am really younger than you, Toni."

This, of course, was all spoken in my presence, for the peculiar pleasure of seeing me writhe. Had I been a little older, I think that I might have been able to manage *Mademoiselle* Marcia. As it was, I could only rage at her or laugh with her as the occasion offered. On this day, I, of course, offered my humble services in whatever they chose to use me for. Antoinette said not a word. It was the entire doing of Marcia that we were forced into a walk. We went down by the river, where Aunt Marcia wished that we were in a canoe; we went back through the forest, where she wished for wings; we climbed two gentle ranges of hills, and here she found a tree with a comfortable spread of shade beneath it and soft new grass with waves of gleaming ripples running through it. There she flounced herself down.

"I shall not budge," said Aunt Marcia. "Yonder is a perfectly good road to the house. You may send a carriage back here for me when you arrive at the stables. Now scatter along, the pair of you and let me rest. I would like to wring the neck of the person who chose a walk for a way to destroy this lovely day."

246

This, of course, was the way of Marcia Gerardin. No one expected her to be logical.

"I'll stay with you, then," said Antoinette.

"Toni!" Aunt Marcia exclaimed. "Where is your breeding? Do you wish to send the poor young man in alone?"

I declared that I would be enchanted to jog in to the château and come back with a carriage for them.

"Don't be so proper and gracious, Jean," Aunt Marcia insisted, frowning on me. "I shall never approve of you until you learn to make me furiously angry. If you were *Monsieur,* what would he say?"

These questions about my father, like so many barbed darts, she never wearied of casting at me.

"I have not the slightest idea," I said, feebly retreating from this virago.

"If you don't know, I'll tell you," Aunt Marcia stated. "Shall I tell you, Jean?"

"If you wish," I responded, growing wretched and casting a guilty glance at Antoinette.

She paid not the slightest attention to *Mademoiselle* Marcia, however. She always regarded her aunt as a sort of amusing toy, full of clownish antics, never to be taken seriously. I could not understand why Antoinette seemed to tower above Marcia — even physically, although she was so slender, and not four inches above five feet.

"Very well," said Marcia Gerardin, "since you wish me to tell you what *Monsieur* would say, I shall do it." She sat up a little straighter and lifted her head. She dropped a hand upon one hip and smiled at Antoinette. Surely *Monsieur* had never shown either of them a single touch of the ironic, cruel side of his nature, and yet this was a very good imitation of the wicked smile of his which still haunts me in my dreams.

"You have chosen to walk out, *Mademoiselle* Gerardin," she said. "Therefore, I shall wait until you are ready to walk in again." Here she bubbled into laugher, but Antoinette watched her seriously.

"That is why I love that man," Marcia declared. "He is so apt to do an uncomfortable thing. Now run along, the pair of you. I want to be alone." She lay down with her fat arms folded beneath her head.

"Shall I go, indeed?" asked Antoinette.

"Heavens, Toni," Aunt Marcia answered, "are you afraid of the boy now that you are about to become his mother?" She waved us away.

Antoinette hesitated another instant, and then, with a shrug of her shoulders, she was walking at my side on the way to the château. From this hilltop we could see the broad roof lifting among the trees, but it was a good two miles away and all between were green-faced farmlands and noble woods.

"Aunt Marcia has not offended you?" Antoinette asked as we went down the slope.

"I am very fond of her," I assured her. "I believe she knows it and teases me because she knows that she can."

"There is a German proverb about that," answered Antoinette. "She likes you immensely because you puzzle her so much. That's one reason. She likes to be mystified."

I could not help laughing. "As a matter of fact," I said, "I feel transparent when I am near her. She is always reading me as easily as though I were done into print."

Antoinette shook her head. "She usually gives that air of assurance," she agreed. "But as a matter of fact she can't fit together the two Jean Limousins. Neither can I. We spend a great deal of time gossiping about you, Jean."

"That is flattering."

"Is it? But do you know what sort of a person I expected to find in you?"

"Please tell me."

"I expected a tigerish look and a wild eye."

"But why?"

"Naturally, after the story of how you had gone storming across Canada, tossing men around as though they were paper dolls."

"Is that it? Well, Antoinette, I shall tell you the story of it in all the details, someday. Then you will see that I did nothing extraordinary . . . except the things that were extraordinarily foolish. I give you my word for that."

"If you do that, I shall be forced to believe you."

"Do! There is no other Jean Limousin than this one you have seen at the château . . . a very quiet and simple person."

"But so melancholy, Jean."

I looked askance at her. We had entered a wood of maples, and the dappling shadows of the young leaves poured across her as she walked. She was looking at me with such a gentle and quiet interest that she took my breath and made me a little giddy. She was not one of those pretty creatures whose youth is half their beauty. Age could never dim her loveliness, and this nearness to her, and her kind and pitying eye, were an intoxication. I found myself breathing internal resolutions that I would say or do no foolish thing.

"If I am a little silent," I tried to explain, "it is not because I am sad, but because I am not naturally very full of talk. Here at the château, all the years, I led a very quiet life, you see."

"Tell me of that," she urged. "Will you tell me about your boyhood, Jean? The moment I saw you, I wondered just what sort of a *little* boy you had been."

"You know," I said, "that children learn to talk by being with playmates of their own age. One does not chatter to the elders so easily."

"That is true," said Antoinette. "But there were *some* playmates for you?"

"Company came very seldom. It was too far to the village, and the children of the families who worked for *Monsieur* . . . well, *Monsieur* has certain ideas of caste . . . which I, for one, do not agree with."

"Ah, yes," Antoinette signed. "It must have been a lonely life for you, poor Jean."

"No, no, I was rarely lonely. At the time I suppose that I thought it was a lonely existence. I wanted playmates sometimes. But on the whole it was a beautiful, happy life. Now, these woods are very charming, are they not? They have grown more pleasant since I was a youngster, of course, but I have another memory of them in which they seemed like glorious giants. The shadows were so black that they left a stain. The sun that dropped through the branches was gold. One could catch handfuls of it!"

She laughed out of pure pleasure. "That is delightful, Jean! I did not dream that you were such a happy youngster."

"Did you not? I can tell you that this was a great fairyland. The château was a place of mystery and darkness that had grown straight out of the heart of a story book. I did not dream of other things. It filled my imagination."

"To every detail?"

"To every one."

"The ogre, Jean?"

"One does not miss such defects in a story," I said, remembering with a little shiver that there had been an ogre, indeed.

"And the fairy princess, Jean?"

"Ah, yes. She was here. If you could have

seen her, Antoinette, how you would have loved her."

I stopped and touched her arm. Speaking to her, indeed, all the sorrow was quite gone from those old days. All was washed pure, just as the rain washes the air and leaves it clean for the sunset to pour it full of rose and gold. The sadness and the sweetness of that other life fell suddenly about me, like glorious music and a shower of rose petals.

Antoinette had paused, too, with a sympathetic light in her eyes.

"She was not so beautiful as you are," I said, peering into her face. "She was a little smaller. She was not so queenly and so strong, but she came out of heaven and kept the glory about her."

"But who was the fairy princess, Jean?"

I had been thinking of myself of ten years before, and thinking so vividly that it was no more than a charming story in which I had been a character. This question put me to a sudden sense of pain, and I stammered: "It was my dear mother, Antoinette." And I walked on hastily.

# Chapter Twenty-Eight

# The Enchanted Forest

I had a great contempt for myself because this rush of grief had so nearly unmanned me. I could have beaten my hands together for shame, and I stole a glance at Antoinette, as soon as I was able, to see what was in her face. Upon my honor, there was nothing but tenderness there. She knew that I was looking at her, and therefore she said quietly: "I am sorry for this, Jean."

When I saw that she was so sincere about it, I could not help stopping again. Do you think that I was very Gallic and explosive and sentimental? However, there are certain things that need to be put into words, and I had never talked of this. So, as we faced one another, I said: "You mean it, Antoinette. And you are filled with gentleness and kindness. Someday I want to talk to you about her."

"With all my heart, Jean."

"Come," I said, "let us walk along. I feel a little choked."

I took her arm, and we went on. I hardly knew what I did, but I was overwhelmed with the sense of joy because I had found this girl to whom I could talk. Consider — if you wonder at me — that I had never had a friend to whom I could open my heart. I shall try to put down what I can remember of the things we said. First:

"I like you, Antoinette."

"I am very glad," she replied.

"If you had smiled or chuckled at me, you would have stabbed me to the heart."

"My dear Jean," she said, "you make me very happy . . . and yet very sad, too. Why is that?"

I paused again, wondering at her.

"Is it so with you? And with me, also. I am so full of happiness that it seems as though all the joy out of my life had been gathered and poured together to flood through my body and my brain. There is an ache of sadness in my throat. And yet, Antoinette, I think that I have never seen such a beautiful day."

"Why have you locked up this self of yours, dear Jean? Why have you never let me see you before?"

"Because this self never lived until I took your arm and walked with you through this enchanted forest, Antoinette. So enchanted, that only to utter your name is a wild joy to me. Is not everything in the world beautiful today?"

"Look," she said. "See that silly squirrel fluffing his tail up and down and barking at us. Why is he so excited? And how his eyes shine."

"Why, he is saying in the clearest words . . . be happy! Be happy! Be happy! Do you hear it?"

"I do now, of course. It is perfectly clear."

"I trust that we shall never reach the château, Antoinette. Just to walk on like this . . . I am bewildered with excitement. Are you?"

"Ah, Jean, I think I know. It is the fragrance of these violets . . . such a cold, small, exquisite fragrance."

"That is it."

"Shall we pick some?"

"No, no, no! For if we pause . . . if we do anything but walk steadily along, not too fast . . . the enchantment will break. I am afraid of that."

256

"Perhaps you are right. How everything smiles at us, Jean. Do you not feel a kindness even for that great white cloud so poured full of sun? Do you see it?"

"It is beautiful. And the very smell of all the wet, growing things in the woods is different today."

"Is it not? I feel, somehow . . . just around the corner of my mind . . . as though I could understand everything today."

"And I! Is it not wonderful? What is in your mind is in mine. What you think is my thought. What you feel is in my heart! How delightful it is to be with you, Antoinette!"

"Let us not pause to wonder at it . . . or then it may all disappear. It is like living in a dream and knowing that one must waken."

"We shall not. We shall fight away the dull old world that we have just escaped from. Shall we not?"

"Unless it is too beautiful to last."

"It cannot be. It is a sin to think that!"

"And yet we were both sad, a little time ago."

"It was the thought of my dear mother. And yet it is as if she led us into this happiness."

"It is a ghostly thing, as though her spirit were in the air beside us."

"How beautiful your hand is, Antoinette."

"It is only an everyday hand, Jean."

"No, it is part of this enchantment. When I touch it, my heart leaps!"

"And mine. Why is it?"

And, as we spoke, stumbling joyously down a path that perhaps I had walked a thousand times before, but which now seemed as strange as a vision of beauty, it brought us suddenly to the last thin screen of trees, and beyond them we saw, solemn and tall, the strong walls of the Château Limousin, with the big windows looking down at us.

We stopped with a shock.

"It is the end, Jean?" she whispered.

We had shrunk back to the shelter of a tree, and somehow, as I looked down at her, at her great, sad, lighted eyes, at her lips, grown pale like all her face — I cannot tell how it was that she was in my arms and I was kissing her. She was straining away from me with only a faint strength, and I was sobbing with a broken breath: "I love you, Antoinette! I love you! And you love me! Love is the enchantment."

Now, when sense came back to me, it

came as suddenly as the day comes into a blackened room when the wind waves the drawn curtain aside. Blinded by the sense of what I had done, I stepped back from her. I waited wretchedly, oh, so filled with guilt, to hear her denounce me. She only leaned a hand against the trunk of the tree, and with the other hand pressed to her heart she looked down to the ground. I covered my eyes with a groan, and, when I looked up again, she was gone.

I did not attempt to follow. There was a fallen log near me that had not yet been cleared away by the woodsmen. On that I sat down and took my head between my hands to try to puzzle out this wilderness into which I had gone, carrying the betrothed of *Monsieur* with me. If, indeed, I *had* carried her with me. Or was it only a headlong impulse of the moment that had made her seem to agree with me, whereas she had been at all times master of herself and her emotion?

When I thought of her, as I sat there with my head in my hands, I was sure that she was filled with rage and scorn. Walking at her side through the forest she had seemed like a happy child with me. At this distance of thinking, I could see her only as the bride of *Monsieur,* full of wisdom, full of strength, a proper wife for him. And she, who had trusted herself so completely to the son of her betrothed, had been so shamed by him.

Here I could not endure the agony for another moment. I sprang up and hurried to the stables, where I took a carriage at once and drove at a wild pace up the road toward that spot where Marcia Gerardin had been inspired by the devil to send the pair of us off together.

She was sound asleep, or she pretended to be sound asleep, and I had to shout again and again from the road where my horses were dancing and fretting on the reins, before she sat up and then came to me. When she got in beside me, I suddenly wished that I had never wakened her, for she decided upon more tormenting, and never paused on the way back. I made the horses fly. Even so the way was long.

Then: "Have you lost your tongue? Can you only say . . . 'Yes, *mademoiselle* . . . no, *mademoiselle*'?"

"I am sorry, *mademoiselle*."

"Look at me, Jean."

"I dare not. The horses would flip us into the ditch in a moment."

"Would they do so? I know what it is."

"What is it, then?"

"You have quarreled with Toni. Well, I shall never stop plaguing her until I find out all about it."

In spite of myself, a groan came from my lips. And she — oh, there was a very devil of penetration in that woman! — she said to me: "Draw in the horses, Jean."

"I cannot," I insisted.

"I shall put my hands on the reins, then."

"Ah, well." I drew back those racing horses to an easy, jogging trot.

"Now, my boy," Aunt Marcia said, very serious and frowning, "what the devil have you done?"

I give her exact words. She was apt to be shockingly rough.

"Heaven knows," I sighed. "I cannot talk."

"So . . . so . . . so. You have actually dared to be indiscreet, Jean!"

"*Mademoiselle*," I said, trembling violently, "I beg you to let me drive on to the château and leave you. I cannot speak of. . . ."

"Of this frightful thing? How terrible it must have been, Jean. The hideous thought comes upon me that you may even have attempted to kiss the hand of Toni. Is it that?"

*"Mademoiselle!"*

"Or that you have actually kissed her lips?"

I could not speak. I was blinded with self-hatred and disgust.

"Dear me," said Aunt Marcia, "what a frightful crime."

Will you believe that she broke into a great laughter that at least served the purpose of keeping her dumb until we reached the château. That laughter never died out, but it came in separate strong waves. One of them caught her as she dismounted from the carriage and sent her staggering up the steps to the door of the house.

# Chapter
# Twenty-Nine

# Lafitte

You may guess that I had no ardent desire to hurry into the château after these bewildering events and this strange conduct on the part of myself, to say nothing of the unusual behavior of *Mademoiselle* Marcia. I was very pleased when, as I went in at last, I was told by a servant that Lafitte wished to see me at my first convenience, that he was in the library. I went there to find him, of course. To my terror and surprise, I found that Antoinette was already with the secretary. I would have withdrawn at once, but Lafitte seized on me at once. He had been showing some bindings to *Mademoiselle* Gerardin, and he came straight for me with a volume open in his hand.

"I have been waiting to see you, *Monsieur* Limousin," he said. "I have been waiting very eagerly, hoping that I could talk to you before I start for the train."

"The train?" I asked. "Oh, has *Monsieur* sent you off on some matter of business?"

"I wished to speak with you," said Lafitte, "so that you could inform *Monsieur* when he returns that I have gone."

"Some relative is sick, Lafitte?" I asked sympathetically.

He smiled a wry smile. "It is not that, *monsieur*. But I feel that I cannot remain in the château after the affairs of last night."

I could have choked the fool for saying so much in the presence of Antoinette. I drew him farther into the corner of the room and remarked softly that such language was extremely indiscreet in the presence of a third person. At this, he colored a little, and then announced, with his chin raised, that he did not know whether or not it was his duty to let everyone know what he had heard, what he had seen, and what he had cause to suspect.

Quite at sea with fury, despair — and amusement — I was irritated at the unsuspected pig-headed honesty of this Puritan. I was in despair when I considered what the results of such scandalous gossip might be, and I was really amused when I saw how completely in error this good man

264

was. Consulting nothing but his conscience, he was about to commit a really important crime against *Monsieur* and me. I could not help saying: "Why did you not communicate this decision to *Monsieur* this morning?"

He winced a little; he was a thoroughly honest fellow. "It was not because I feared *Monsieur*," he explained at last, "but it is my habit never to announce an important decision in the morning. That is a testy period. I always wait until the afternoon has brought matters around to normal."

"It is a wholly admirable idea," I remarked. "Now will you tell me frankly what it is that you feel yourself called upon to communicate to the world?"

He cleared his throat: "I do not wish to embarrass you, *Monsieur* Limousin."

I wondered how my father could have made such an error in employing this man of conscience.

"I had rather be embarrassed before my face than behind my back," I said, growing a little hot.

"I have no intention of dodging behind coverts in order to harm the family of Limousin," he said.

I could not help breaking out: "You are wise, *monsieur*. It might be a dangerous proceeding. To come back to the matter of last night, let me tell you that I can guess what is in your mind."

"I presume that you can, sir."

"It is this. You believe that I left my room last night, entered the chamber of my father, and made an attack upon him."

He flushed when I put the matter so bluntly to him. "I feel," he said, "that the noises I heard were not made by the overturning of a table that had books upon it."

"Ten thousand devils!" I exclaimed. "Of course not! Come, come, Lafitte, you realize that there are times when it is necessary for a white lie to be told, do you not?"

"I am in the habit of telling the truth," declared Lafitte. "I have not the energy to build up elaborate inventions."

There is always something frightfully irritating about extreme virtue. I had the greatest desire in the world to break the neck of this stiff-backed man. I could not help remembering, also, what the reactions of *Monsieur* would be, if he heard of such a tale going the rounds of the countryside.

"Do you realize," I asked, "that such a report as you may make would perhaps have great consequences?"

"I do fully realize it."

"Do you realize that, whatever really

happened behind the door of my father's room, he was not seriously injured, nor was I, and that in such a conflict, if there had been one, there must have been some outward evidences left? Above all, you have my solemn oath, which I shall take in any manner you desire, that your presumption is wrong. What *did* happen in that room, I see no reason why the world should not know, as well as the cause of my entering it. It is simply a whim of *Monsieur*'s."

"I believe," said the rigid Lafitte, "that *Monsieur*'s door onto the balcony . . . the same balcony which your chamber opens upon . . . was found forced from the outside this morning."

I was astonished that *Monsieur* could have allowed such a peculiar bit of evidence to remain for the world to see. More than that, I was thunderstruck that he should allow the rumor a chance of spreading when there was an innocent truth to explain away everything. He knew that the entire countryside had already been scandalized by the report of a quarrel between *Monsieur* and his son, which had sent the son scattering wildly away into the world. Behind this, there was the more distant and tragic legend of Hubert

Guillaume of which it was only known that the boy had committed suicide after a quarrel with his father. Yet, in the face of such a scandal at a time when he was using his utmost endeavors to bring about a marriage with beautiful Antoinette Gerardin, he faced all these dangers rather than expose to the knowledge of the world the attack that Pierre Reynal had made upon him.

"Listen to me, Lafitte," I said, more and more despairing. "It is at least reasonable to wait until *Monsieur* returns to the house."

At this he shuddered. "I tell you, *Monsieur* Limousin," he said with a great emotion and entirely too loud a voice, "I could not be persuaded to spend another night in this house! I believe that I am not a coward, but this is a thing which I fear to do."

"Lafitte," I said through my teeth, "your voice is reaching the ears of *mademoiselle*."

He shrugged his broad shoulders; his virtue was making him more aggressive every moment. My irritation grew, also. The pulse of my heart was so great that it swayed my entire body.

"I am sorry for that," he stated, "but I really do not know that it is honest for me to leave the château before I have opened the entire matter to her ears as far as I know it."

This was really too much, as you will agree. Still, I kept myself stiffly in hand and managed to control my voice, also.

"*Monsieur* Lafitte, you are really going a great length in a matter upon which you have no positive evidence."

"*Monsieur* Limousin, since I have come to the château, I have closed my eyes upon a great deal. I have endeavored to see nothing except the work that lay before me in the course of every day. I have endeavored to keep from dwelling upon certain odd bits of evidence. For instance, that *Monsieur* has been twice married, on both occasions to young and very beautiful women."

"Will you keep down your voice, Lafitte?"

I have no doubt that Antoinette would have left the room before this, if we had not been standing so near to the door that her withdrawal would have been exceedingly marked. As it was, she had already gone to the farthest corner of the room, and there she sat with her face half turned away from us, pretending an interest in a book that was in her lap, and yet the pages never turned. For the voice of Lafitte had a sharp, nasal, American quality that made his words extraordinarily clear and gave his voice a great carrying quality.

I think that Lafitte hardly heard my last protest. He was filled with a headlong excitement, now, that carried him blindly ahead. He was one of those muscular, deep-chested types who make physical culture a part of their religion — the care of the body with the care of the mind and the soul — and now he was fairly expanding with virtuous indignation and suspicion. He went on in a louder voice than ever: "Both of the wives of *Monsieur* died suddenly. A young son by his first marriage was found with a bullet through his head . . . sent there by his own hands, it was said. You yourself *Monsieur* Limousin. . . ."

"Lafitte," I said, beginning to view him through a red mist, "I ask you earnestly to leave this room with me that we may talk alone. And in the meantime, if my solemn oath to you isn't. . . ."

"*Monsieur*," said Lafitte, "did you speak of your oath?"

"I did."

In this day, when the minds of men turn with a careless curiosity into all the corners of thought, and when religion is little more than a dreamy habit with most, it is difficult to remember that, a scant half generation before, religion was a blind passion in many breasts. I say this to explain the singular bluntness of Lafitte's next remark. For he said: "I do not know, *monsieur*, what oath would be of value from a man who has no real belief in a Creator and a just God!"

The double irritation of this foolish talk on the one hand and of Antoinette as an audience on the other hand had worked me up to a higher pitch than I dreamed. I thought that I still had myself well in hand at the very instant that my patience was completely gone. Now my passion burst out like a fire that reaches dry leaves. There must have been a warning of what was coming in my face, for Lafitte, with a sudden exclamation, leaped back and put up his hands to defend himself. He might as well have erected a paper screen against a cannonball, for my fury had magnified me as I have heard that insanity magnifies the mad.

I leaped in at him, drove my fist through his warding arms, and reached his face with such force that I felt my knuckles bite through flesh and grind against bone. Lafitte was flung from his feet against the wall by this terrible blow and then pitched to the floor upon his face.

# Chapter Thirty

# A Young Tiger

When I recovered my senses — for such a devilish outbreak is like a wave of senselessness — I was holding Lafitte by the nape of the neck as a bull terrier holds a vanquished foe and shakes it. I was telling him harshly to stand on his feet again because I was not yet done with him. Then, as my wits came back and my eyes cleared, I saw Antoinette, standing pale and still in the far corner of the room, and old Guilbert who had just entered, looking on with a face of horror. I had only one controlling impulse — that was to get myself and my mischief away from the sight of Antoinette as quickly as possible. I lifted Lafitte in my arms. Although he was a sturdy chunk of a man, my passion still lent me power, and I hurried with a light step out of the library, carrying my burden.

Behind me, as I went, I heard the voice of Guilbert break out: "Ah, it is the ghost of *Monsieur!*"

I took Lafitte into the next chamber — the dining room — and began to wash his face with water from a decanter. The blow had struck him beside the temple, splitting the skin. Besides, from his fall to the floor, his mouth was badly cut and already swelling. There was an instant when I feared that I had killed him, but then I was able to feel the flutter of his heart, very small and weak. All the time I was muttering to myself: "I have brought down the devil. All is lost. All is lost."

Now that Lafitte had so far recovered that he was beginning to open his eyes and groan, I picked him up again and went with him up the two flights of stairs to his room. I met a servant on my way up, and the fellow shrank against the wall and gaped at me. I presume that it was an odd sight to watch a man no larger than myself, running lightly up a flight of stairs with such a burden as I then supported.

Hysteria has made men do stranger things. I remember a blacksmith who told me how his infant daughter had fallen into a shallow run of water and her body lodged under a culvert that was no more than few stout two-by-fours, nailed down with strong spikes. He tore those heavy timbers away with his naked hands and drew her out, still living.

I called to the servant as I went past him to send for a doctor as fast as a horse could fly. Then I went on with Lafitte to his room. His trunk stood packed in the corner of the floor, surrounded by hand luggage. I remember the scrupulous neatness with which this poor fellow had put the chamber to rights before he left it. Neatness was to him one of the chief moral virtues, and disorder a sin fit for the devil.

Laying him on his bed, I found that his eyes were now wide open, but they stared up at me without the slightest recognition. He began to groan in a terrible way and laid a hand against his bruised temple.

A hand tapped at the door.

"What is it? Who is it?" I called out. "Is it the doctor?"

I had sent for the doctor hardly half a minute before, but my brain was in such a whirl that I took no heed of the passage of time. Every second was a long minute.

"No," said the voice of Antoinette Gerardin, "it is only I, Jean."

First, like the foolish little boy who has broken the window but stoutly denies it, although he knows it must be discovered in another moment, I thought of keeping her from the room. Then, with a groan, I went to admit her.

She was still pale, but she was not staring at me.

"I want to know if I can help," she said. "How is *Monsieur* Lafitte now?"

"You may see him," I said, and pointed to the bed.

I thought that she shrank a little as she went past me, but she sat down on the side of the bed and took the wrist of unlucky Lafitte in the tips of her fingers in a business-like way that made me feel more helpless than ever. She replaced his hand at his side.

"He will die!" I exclaimed.

She looked up to me with a face blank with thought, and then down at my hand. "Your hand is bleeding, Jean," was all she said. "You had better tie it up."

I was pushed into a figurative corner, one might say, and told to be quiet, so I stood by and watched her dip a towel in cold water, wring it out, and make a swift, neat bandage around the head of Lafitte. His groaning, which had continued with every other breath all this while, began to diminish, although his eyes were as horribly empty and glassy as ever.

"I think it will be well to get him to

bed," said Antoinette.

"There is a hope for him, Antoinette?"

"Oh, yes."

How very calm she was. She opened his trunk while I worked his clothes off. She found and tossed to me his nightclothes and continued to take out what things he might need and arrange them in the drawers of the big chest in the corner of the room. When I had him between the sheets at last, she came back again and sat down beside him, her fingers on his pulse once more.

"Can you bring me some brandy?" she asked.

In three bounds I was down the stairs and back again with a decanter. Then I watched her raise his head gently and pour a dram down his throat. It made him cough and groan more heavily than ever, but, after a moment, both coughing and groaning ceased, and his eyes closed.

"He is dead, Antoinette," I said, clasping my helpless hands together.

"Hush," she replied. "His eyes would not close if he were really dead." She turned and looked at me thoughtfully. "I think that you had better go out into the open air," she suggested.

"I must stay here to do what I can," I

protested. "I cannot leave you to. . . ."

"You must not talk so loudly. See . . . it disturbs him. I think he hears your voice even now. You must leave him, Jean."

I stole down the stairs like a guilty cur. In the lowest hall I encountered Guilbert, and he shrank from me as though I were a wild beast escaped from a cage. I went out under the sky, and looked back upon the heavy walls of the château as though it were a place where a thousand devils lodged.

Sometimes I ran; sometimes I walked. It was dusk when I returned to the château, filled with weakness, very weary, indeed, but with the fiend quite gone from my brain. The first person I encountered was she whom I could most easily face — Marcia Gerardin. She took me by the arm and led me into a room and made me sit in a chair by the fire.

"So!" exclaimed *Mademoiselle* Marcia. "So!" She brought me a glass of wine and made me swallow it, and then she sat down, scowling at me. "You have distinguished yourself, Jean."

I was full of despair instantly. "He is dying . . . he is dead."

"No."

"But the doctor has come?"

"Yes."

"And he gives no hope?"

"About this Lafitte? Do you think that I care what happens to that dark-minded man? Tush!" She waved poor Lafitte into the outer darkness.

"Then," I begged her, "then what, *Mademoiselle* Gerardin?"

"Then what?" she asked, mimicking me savagely. "Then nothing . . . except the devil himself. Oh, young madman."

"*Mademoiselle*," I said, "be gentle. I am very sick at heart."

"Why are not young men kept under a rope and bridled?" she asked. "Why are they allowed to remain at large in this fashion? Can you tell me why?"

I stared heavily at her. "There is nothing I can say," I muttered. "There is nothing that I can say, *mademoiselle*."

She stamped her heavy foot upon the floor. "But there is something which you can say," she declared. "You can tell me why you did not knock the fool down before he had had a chance to rattle out all that mischief. Can you explain that to me, Jean?"

"Why should I attempt to speak? I have acted the part of a devil."

"You have acted the part of a ninny. If God gave you so much strength in your hands, why did He not give you enough sense to use it at the right time? But where is that strength of yours?"

She picked up my hand and turned it over. I confess that I was now trembling from head to foot. She tossed my hand away and shook her head.

"I cannot understand," she said. "Unless some people are dry powder that explodes, now and then. Oh, well, I shall never be able to understand, and nothing maddens me more than mystery. As if *Monsieur* were not enough . . . now you?"

"Antoinette. . . ."

"Antoinette?" She mocked me in the same whining tone. "Aye, that is the crux of the trouble. Antoinette. Oh, Jean, how much of a problem you have given me. How much of a problem."

"Ah, but she despises me now."

"Does she? I don't know. I don't know that I care. But, *monsieur*, now what in the fiend's name will the headstrong child take into her head to do? Oh, I wish that I could tell. I wish that I could tell."

At this same unpleasant moment the voice of *Monsieur* sounded in the hall. I felt like the hidden child who hears the ogre entering the room.

"I have wit enough to guess one thing,"

279

said Marcia Gerardin. "Which is that I had better see your father before you do. Go into that room. Leave the door ajar one half inch, so that you will hear."

I should not have done it. It was not gentlemanly or brave — but I sneaked into the next room and left the door exactly as she had bidden me to leave it.

# Chapter
# Thirty-One

# A Coward?

It was a noncommittal little chamber that had no particular purpose in the world. There were a few books in a hanging shelf on the wall; there was a tall mirror framed in coils of a heavy gilded design. From a corner of the ceiling hung a little round bird cage, empty these many years. My mother had once loved this room, partly because it was small, I suppose, and as close an approach to snugness as an apartment in the château could suggest. Besides, there were two great windows, standing side by side and looking to the south. Here she used to love to come with her sewing and sit in the flare of the sun while two little canaries in the cage whistled and throbbed with music or fluttered from perch to perch — glittering jewels of green and gold.

Afterward the room fell under a shadow for that gentle soul. The shadow dropped over it on that day when *Monsieur,* striding into this very chamber, had cast me down at her feet and cried: "You have given me a son like yourself! He is a fool and a coward . . . a coward and a fool . . . like you, Julie!"

This, then, was what sank into my mind, and, as I dropped into a chair, I felt as though *Monsieur* had grown into a vast giant so that the proportions between us were as in that other day when I had given him his first real disgust for me.

I heard *Monsieur* whistling in the hall, the distant voice of *Mademoiselle* Marcia stopping him, then both their voices louder, as she drew him into the other room.

*Monsieur* said: "My dear *Mademoiselle* Gerardin, you look full of mischief. And are you?"

"I am full of news."

"Good news, then?" he asked. "I cannot imagine you in the rôle of the raven."

"I think that you would detest the bearer of ill tidings."

"Do you think so? Well, we all have our eccentricities. But what is the news, by all means. And is it really bad?"

"I think it will hurt like a pinch of the

very devil's fingers."

What a way to break a tale to *Monsieur!*

"I am prepared, *mademoiselle.* I am braced against the shock."

"It begins with your secretary . . . that precious Lafitte."

"So? So?" asked *Monsieur,* with just a trace of emotion in his voice. "He is a dark dog, is he not?"

"He is!" exclaimed Aunt Marcia with the heartiest emphasis. "He decided today that he would leave. He would not even wait for your return."

"Is that all? Is that all? That is nothing. I have never liked his ways. It is an excellent riddance, after all."

"But before he left, he had to give his reasons."

"To you?"

"No, not to me . . . to a more important person."

The voice of *Monsieur,* lifting from its usually well-trained note of politeness, rang through the room: "To Antoinette!"

"Yes," said *Mademoiselle* Gerardin.

My father took a turn through the room. I could hear the crushing of his feet on the rug. The floor quivered a little beneath me, carrying to me some of the nervous tension of *Monsieur*'s own soul.

"Very well," he said, pausing. "Now tell me about it. Tell me everything, if you please."

"I shall tell you everything so far as I know it. Jean had come into the library. . . ."

"Ah, Jean was in it."

How well I knew that purring note of collected wrath.

"Lafitte had wished to speak with him, and Jean came in while Lafitte was showing Antoinette some of your bindings."

"Continue, continue!"

"It came very briefly. Lafitte announced that he was leaving. Jean naturally expressed some wonder. . . ."

"Why did he do that? Why not let the fool go and there an end of it? But pardon me, *mademoiselle*. Continue again, if you please?"

"In another instant, Lafitte was bursting out with a thousand reasons for leaving the château, and among others he said that he was afraid to spend another night beneath this roof, and he added some odd insinuations . . . very odd, *Monsieur*."

"Did Jean stand and allow the dog to say these things?"

"No, no! Jean tried to do what he could

to stop him or to at least make him lower his voice, but, when Lafitte saw that he was being controlled, he was seized with a spasm of conscience that seemed to tell him that he must make the entire world hear what he had to say. Oh, *Monsieur,* a great many crimes are performed in the name of religion."

"Are there not? But all of this fascinates me. What did the rogue have to say?"

"Things that I know you can brush away in a moment. But he began with a great many insinuations, as I said before. And among other things he mentioned the fact that you had been married twice before."

"So? Is that a novel bit of news?"

"And that both of your wives died young."

"The rat . . . ah, *mademoiselle,* the rat to make such an insinuation."

"That one son had committed suicide. I am sorry, but you must know exactly what came to the ear of Antoinette."

"I must, indeed."

"And that another son was driven from your house."

"Sacred devil! Did not Jean close the dog's mouth then?"

"There were some more words, and then

Jean struck this fellow to the floor."

"I thank heaven for it."

"But Lafitte is seriously injured."

"Ah? I wish his neck had been broken!"

"You must understand, *Monsieur*, that Jean seized him as a cat seizes a rat, and Antoinette was a little frightened."

"Do I understand you?" asked *Monsieur* in a sharply changed voice.

"I think that you do. It must have been a frightful thing to see. He almost killed Lafitte with a single blow of his hand. One of the servants, entering, cried out at the sight of Jean's face . . . 'The ghost of *Monsieur!*' And that was it."

"And Antoinette saw all of this?"

"She did. I have the story from her, of course."

"In all this detail?"

"And more, but nothing of importance, I believe."

"What effect does it have upon her?"

"An effect which will not please you, I am afraid."

"She is frightened?"

"Yes, and more than that. I am sorry to tell you, *Monsieur*, but she says that she feels we should leave the château tomorrow."

My father began to pace up and down

through the room again, and a shudder passed through me with the sound of every footfall.

"A delightful tangle. A delicious affair," he murmured at last. "Where is Antoinette now?"

"In the room of Lafitte. She has been nursing him. The man was badly injured, *Monsieur*, although the doctor says that he will recover. But only with the most careful attention."

"But tell me, did Jean allow her to go to that man?"

"She went of her own accord. He could not control her. She is very headstrong, *Monsieur*."

"And Jean, *mademoiselle*. Can you tell me where he is?"

She raised her voice a little. "I don't know. In the library, I believe."

I did not wait to hear any more, but, using that hint, I fled to the library, having barely time to sit down and compose myself when *Monsieur* entered. He came over to me without speaking and stood by my chair, smiling down at me, combing his beard with all of a cold-blooded devil in his face.

"*Monsieur?*"

"I am about to find out whether or not

you have ruined my life, Jean," said my father.

"I wished to tell you, *Monsieur*," I said, rising, "that. . . ."

"I have heard the entire story."

"If I displayed some savagery, *Monsieur*, remember that I was provoked."

"Jean, if you wished to strike, and strike for me, why did you not send a bullet through his heart when the cur first opened his lips about me? Now there is nothing left to me but this." He looked about him with a gesture. "I must go to face her," he said, "and I had rather face a leveled row of guns. But in ten minutes, Jean, I shall know whether or not you are what I have always suspected . . . a fatal poison in my life."

He turned his back on me and went to the door, but there he paused and cleared his throat a little. He opened the door and shut it again. It is my conviction that he was rehearsing in his mind what he would say to her. He threw a murmur over his shoulder to me.

"You have seen her. Is she excited or is she calm?"

"She is calm, *Monsieur*."

"Ah, that is worse . . . that is so much the worse."

He made still another pause. This was the man of iron, and yet I assure you that he was trembling from head to foot as, at last, he jerked the library door open and quickly started out into the hall.

I listened to his steps for a moment. I was seized with such a chill that I stretched out my numbed hands to the fire and bathed them in the heat. Upon the interview with Antoinette would depend the interview that was to come next — between my father and me.

# Chapter Thirty-Two

# The Interview

I could not have remained quietly in that room while the talk went on between *Monsieur* and Antoinette. That interview would decide whether or not my father was to meet me in tolerance or in a mortal passion that might bring to this sad house the most terrible of the tragedies that had occurred within its walls. I could not have remained still. Once I rose and began to move back and forth, but it was impossible for me to do other than one thing — to start for the window of the room of Lafitte, where Antoinette now was — and to which *Monsieur* was going.

You see I did not attempt to excuse myself or veil my actions with an honorable excuse. It was very dishonest. There is nothing more vile than the eavesdropper.

Yet I did not even pause to consider on which side honor lay. I went to the second story as fast as I could and through my room to the balcony upon which my outer doors opened.

The May night was sharp, with the chill of a growing mist in it that promised to give us rain before the morning. All the windows were clotted and clouded with it, and it pressed against my face like a wet, icy hand. It was a grateful touch to my aching head. I hung on the railing of the balcony for a moment, with my head thrown back, letting the chill come against my beating throat as well. Only half the sky was darkened. The stars and a thin edge of moon floated in the other half, with the billowing mist now and again washing half the stars from my sight and then, like the wave of a curtain, giving them back to me again.

Then I turned toward the lighted windows of Lafitte's room, just above the chamber of *Monsieur.* There the balcony ended, and a heavy shaft of ornamental stonework descended like a support for the balcony from above. On the massive scrollwork of this shaft a child could have climbed with perfect safety, even on a dark, wet night like this, so I worked my way in a trice up to the windows of Lafitte. With my feet firmly braced on the uppermost scroll of the stone I was in a position to keep my head between the two windows, and in this manner I could peer in from time to time, while hearing everything that was spoken, as long as it was in a voice loud enough to carry above the noise of the wind.

*Monsieur* was not yet there, and, rapidly as I had climbed, I knew that he must have paused once or twice to consider his lines again before the critical moment. I cannot tell you how much this meant to me — I, who had seen him in terrible situations before this, but never in such a place that he was at a loss for a right word.

I did not hear the tap at the door, but I saw Antoinette lift her head, and I saw her face change. *Monsieur* had at last arrived. He came in at once, and I could not help a smile of admiration. He had so thoroughly mastered the tremendous passion of yearning and fear that I knew to be in him, that he was able to nod and smile at her in a very brisk, friendly fashion. At the same time, he went forward to the bed and looked down at Lafitte. A gesture of the hand sent the nurse from the room.

In all that followed, I saw *Monsieur* at his

best and at his most dangerous. When I consider now the consummate tact he used to this girl, whom he loved with all his heart and who had already announced her intention of leaving the château — and his life — when I think of this, I wonder that he did not enter into political life of some sort, for I am sure that his success in it would have been very great.

He considered Lafitte very seriously, at first. The poor secretary was now in a wretched condition, his head still bandaged, his eyes sometimes closed and sometimes open, but never with a light of sense in them. He moved continually and needed close watching. Antoinette had remained with him because her voice had a quiet influence over the delirious man, whereas the others had to use force to control him.

"The doctor's report is a very serious statement," said *Monsieur*.

"It is, François," said Antoinette.

"Ah, ah," said *Monsieur*. "It is a very pleasant thing for me to hear you speak that name. Particularly now that I am to hear your voice so seldom."

If he was calm — at least in his appearance — it was nothing compared with the perfect ease of Antoinette. She looked up at him as she said: "You have talked with

Aunt Marcia, then?"

"I've just finished talking with her."

"Well," Antoinette said in her slow way, "I hope that I have said nothing unfair. It is so easy for a girl to be a haphazard little fool. But I have been thoroughly frightened, François."

"Is that possible? I admit that it is an ugly mess throughout. This Lafitte . . . ah, well, one cannot hate such a fellow. I think he said no more than he honestly believed."

Antoinette leaned back in her chair until her head rested against the wall, watching *Monsieur* — not boldly, but with thought. She was so fearless and so honest that one could see her reaching for the truth, always. By so much was she beyond all the other men and women of the world.

"It is not that I have closed my mind to what you may have to say, François," she said. "I am only wretched because I have had such a panic. If you wish to explain. . . ."

*Monsieur* permitted himself to smile on her. "You are marvelously honest and fair, Antoinette. But I don't think that I shall try to defend myself. Lafitte has condemned me with ridiculous universality. Well, my dear, perhaps he is right in spirit, even if he is wrong in facts. He accused me

. . . of what? Of murdering one son and driving another from the château. Of destroying two wives because . . . who knows why?"

"*Monsieur*, I never could have entertained such suspicions of you. No, never, of course."

"I know that you could not," my father replied very gravely. "You are too wise and too just to do such a thing, Antoinette, but you gave your ear to the thing behind his words. And in that I admit that you are very right. Indeed, I hesitate to review a great deal of my life, even with my own eyes."

"Do you, truly?" she asked, wondering at his candor almost as greatly as I, crouched outside the window, watching this battle of the giants, wondered at it.

"There are periods . . . years at a time," *Monsieur* stated calmly, "I like to keep buried in my memory. They are black times, you may be sure. After all, it would have been very difficult to season my nature with much of the saint. Very difficult, Antoinette. If I were now what I was two or three years ago, I should never have been able to come to you so calmly. I could not sit still and acquiesce in such a loss. I would have been like a wild devil in the château, I assure you. In fact, my dear, I am astonished at my own mildness at this moment."

She, of course, could never read signs that she had not seen before, but I, who was familiar with every possible expression of *Monsieur*, knew by a spasmodic opening and closing of his hands that a devil was torturing him. Yet he could speak of his mildness with apparent truth. How great a man was *Monsieur*.

"And I am surprised, also," she said.

"But I have had a great lesson," said *Monsieur*. "My last outbreak of temper sent my dear Jean flying away from the château, and there was a time during which I feared that I had lost him forever. At last I won him back to me. However, that was a fright that has helped me to school my bad temper."

Antoinette watched him with the most eager interest. It was plain that every instinct was working in his favor now because, by making a few adroit admissions, he seemed to nullify the force of all the rest of the accusations of Lafitte, either explicit or implied. By freely accepting a partial blame, he seemed to make the importance of his sins evaporate. I have seen other men do cleverly diplomatic things, but I have never watched one negotiate half so effectively as *Monsieur*.

"*Monsieur,* if I return to Gerardin . . . ," she began.

"I shall start with Jean for a little jaunt around the world. That is all. In a few years I suppose that I shall be as much recovered as most from heartbreak. You see that I do not sham, Antoinette. I do not think that many men have the power in their dull souls to love any woman as I love you . . . but it will not kill me if I lose you."

"You would not let us begin again as rather close friends . . . but not with this sudden thought of marriage."

"Forgive me, Antoinette. To be beaten, to be forced to surrender after a hard battle . . . yes, I can conceive of that. But to live between day and day, wondering . . . 'Does she care more? Does she care less?' That, Antoinette, would be impossible for me."

She dropped her head a little and pondered. "I believe you," said Antoinette. "I do think that you are fond of me, François. And I dread making any quick decision. May I take another day?"

She was not watching him at that instant, so that *Monsieur* allowed some of his joy to spring into his eyes. It was a ragged lightning flash. I did not wait to see anything more, but I climbed down as I had come, as secretly as possible, and regained my room. What *Monsieur* would do at the end of the day might be as violent as what he would have done on this day if she had not put off the decision. In any case, the blow would fall upon me, because it was due to me that Lafitte had burst into such full cry.

I was about as thoroughly unnerved as I had ever been in my life. In the past two or three hours there had been a lifetime of joy, shame, fear, and sorrow mingled. In the family of Limousin one was forced to control such emotions. Let me say that *Monsieur* appeared at the dinner table more suave than ever, and his astonishing candor surpassed all else. It seemed impossible that one could go so far as he did.

He said openly to me: "Jean, you are to understand . . . it may keep you from embarrassment . . . that Antoinette and I are in a state of suspense, and our engagement discontinues." After which he went on with the ordinary current of small talk.

I could not help feeling that he had benefited himself again in the eyes of Antoinette. Keen as she was, even she could not be expected to look through this mask of blunt, apparent honesty to the keener evil behind it. It is easy enough to detect the ordinary villain — Iago escapes.

# Chapter Thirty-Three

# "To Die for Him!"

The first thing in the morning, of course, I went to see the condition of my victim. I found Lafitte weak and pale, but his wits had come back to him. The effects of the blow promised to do no more than to keep him in bed for a few more days. He was so swollen and poisoned with malice that, when I spoke to him, he would not speak to me for some time. But at length this muscular person said: "It was a trick, *Monsieur* Jean. Otherwise, I should have been able to block that blow."

Considering all that blow had meant, I was a little shocked and a great deal amused by this response from Lafitte. However, to find him so much recovered was a huge relief. I should have endured a great deal more from him without attempting any argument. I could not help going to the window and looking at the place where I had played the part of eaves-dropper so shamelessly the night before.

There was a low-lying mist, not suffi-cient wholly to shut away the sun, but transparent and luminous with its light that struck through and made the forest, with all its new, yellow-green leaves, glisten — except in the distance, where the fog was pooled through the woods like thick, white smoke. It was such a day as makes one eager to be out in the open. Certainly I could not have guessed by the face of that morning that the blackest of all the dark chapters of the château was about to be written.

When I left Lafitte, I met Antoinette in the hallway, coming to see her patient — coming, as it seemed to me, with all the beauty of that morning like rose and dew upon her face. It was the first time I had been alone with her since that fateful after-noon of the day before, and I paused to try to find some words for a miserable apology. Then I saw, with bewilderment, that she was as much frightened as I.

I do not feel that I have given you a living picture of Antoinette, but perhaps you have guessed that she had seemed to me second in strength and courage to *Monsieur* alone — yes, able to meet even him upon equal terms. Therefore, when I saw her color change and her eyes widen a little, I was amazed. I said: "Antoinette, I know that you despise me, but will you try to forgive me for yesterday? Will you call it madness and try to forget it?"

What will you say when I tell you that she could not meet my eyes and that she looked down to the hall floor, saying: "I shall think of it as you wish me to, Jean."

I went from her feeling more than ever like a guilty dog, full of sorrow, and yet full of excitement, too — I could not tell why. In the lower hall I had that meeting with *Monsieur* that I had been dreading. He chose to say nothing, but held me with his brilliant eyes while I saw the scorn and dislike and reproaches shadow his face in turn.

He merely said contemptuously at last: "*Mademoiselle* Marcia has gone out for a walk in the woods. I think you had better follow her and offer her your company. Remember that you can help to undo the pretty work which you have done."

"But, *Monsieur*," I cried, "is not *Mademoiselle* Marcia your ally?"

"Stuff!" *Monsieur* spit out. "Do you believe the words she speaks? She is the soul and incarnation of suspicion. She is more filled with the devil than a cup can be filled with poison!"

This was what he chose to say of that apparently simple, outspoken woman whom I liked so very well on account of her honesty. However, I could not deny him. His knowledge of human nature certainly was a great ocean compared to the small pools of my knowledge. I went out obediently to find Aunt Marcia and ask her if she wished for my company.

She was a brisk walker, however, when she chose to step out. The direction she had taken was pointed out to me, but, although I walked on briskly for a good half hour, I did not come on any trace of her. I started back more slowly, convinced that she could not have gone so far, and weaving more deliberately from side to side — from one path to another path. It was well over an hour after I left the house before I caught a glimpse of her, not on any of the roads or paths, but on a hillside down which the breeze was sweeping bright ghosts of mist. She was not alone, but was talking with a tall shadow of a man, the sight of whom sent a shock of fear through me. It was Reynal!

I hurried forward. What he could be saying to her I dared not so much as to try to guess. I lost sight of them as I descended into the hollow. When I came up the hill beyond, I found Marcia, alone, coming down. Reynal, of course, had disappeared. That extra sense that he possessed must have warned him of my approach.

My good-natured *Mademoiselle* Marcia passed me like a cloud without a word of greeting. When I came up to her side, she gave me one eloquent look and with — "If you please, *monsieur*." — she banished me from her.

She went straight back to the house, with me trailing at a miserable distance behind. When she came to the château, she paused and let me come up with her.

"Will you ask Antoinette to come out to me here?" she said coldly.

I could only bow to her and hurry in. What should I do? I rushed to *Monsieur* to tell him.

"She has seen Reynal. I found them talking. Reynal disappeared before I came up, and *mademoiselle* went by me with a face like thunder. She is outside the château, now, and asks me to send Antoinette to her."

*Monsieur,* while I burst out in this fashion, went on with the task of taking out a cigarette and rolling it to the proper softness — because he liked a cigarette that burned freely. Then he lighted it and blew out a thin, blue-brown wisp of smoke as I ended. My father merely said: "If you had come up with Reynal, what would you have done?"

"I am armed, *Monsieur,*" I declared. "I should have killed him as I would kill a wolf!"

"My brave little Jean," *Monsieur* commented, half amused and half contemptuous and half surprised, also. "Would you do so much? Let me tell you this . . . he would not lift a hand to keep you from sending a bullet through his heart. Does not that surprise you?"

I could do nothing but gape at him. Finally I asked: "But now, *Monsieur,* what shall I do?"

"Find Antoinette, of course, as you were told to do, and escort her out to *Mademoiselle* Marcia."

I did as he bade me do. What was the right or the wrong thing to do, I could hardly tell — but I felt, for some odd reason, that in this whirl of entangling rights and duties the simplest thing for me to attempt was to work for the right of *Monsieur*. I found Antoinette curled up in a chair in the library with a great book of old maps in her lap, and her ankles gathered in one slender hand.

"I am marking out the district of Limousin," she explained, smiling up at me.

I told her that her aunt wished to see her and that she was outside the château.

"It is nothing serious, then?" said Antoinette.

"Alas, Antoinette," I could not help answering, "is there anything but seriousness in this sad house of ours?"

I tried to escort her, but she said that she would go alone. I watched her stepping lightly down the hall, and then turned around to find the somber form of *Monsieur* just behind me.

"I should think, Jean," he stated, "that she would make even a cold heart like yours leap. I should think that she would make a timid nature such as yours thunder and rage like white waters." He had his glance fixed upon the bend of the hall around which she had just disappeared.

"I do not speak of her brave, calm soul, Jean," he said. "I do not speak of her wise and understanding mind. Such things are delights to old men like François Limousin. But consider only the beauty of her face, because even a child will love a charming face. Or consider the exquisite workmanship which has been lavished upon her body." Here he combed his glossy, curling beard and allowed the devil in him to smile upon me. "But to a child like you these things remain mysteries, I presume. Learn from me, Jean, that the whole woman is revealed in her hand, and how curved, how tapered and delicate is the hand of Antoinette. Even granting that you are nearly blind to such perfections, still there remains a fragrance of beauty that I should think, in spite of closed eyes, would steal upon the brain and fill you with an ecstasy. Yet there is not even a tinge of color in your face as I speak of her."

I cannot guess why he should have chosen to torment and insult me at this moment of all moments in his life, unless it were, perhaps, that he had a suspicion even then of the truth. This I greatly doubt.

He immediately added: "The time has now come when my fate may rest in your hands, Jean. How much Reynal has said to Marcia I can only guess. For no one can know what is in the mind of Satan . . . even

I cannot guess it. Very well, Jean, you may presume, as I do, that a great deal will bear upon my treatment of you and of Julie. It may be that a few words from you might balance against all that Reynal has said. I cannot force you to speak these few words. But I put myself in your hands, Jean. I put the happiness of your father in your hands. Jean, do what you can for me . . . in charity."

Perhaps even this was acting, but, when he laid his hand on my shoulder and spoke with a tremor in his voice, I suddenly pitied him from the roots of my soul. He left me at once, and I saw him stride down the hall with his head bowed a little as he passed into the library. In that moment I was prepared to die for him.

Do you now wonder, as I do, at the ease with which he had passed from the character of *Monsieur* — terrible, cynical, contemptuous — to the character of my father?

I had hardly a chance to control the great swelling of my heart, which was filled with pity and a will to serve him, when Marcia and Antoinette came into the house and found me.

# Chapter Thirty-Four

# The Torture Chamber

With a single word, *Mademoiselle* Marcia gathered me into their party and conducted us, by an unlucky chance, into that same little chamber where the empty canary cage of my mother still hung. I could see that there was trouble ahead. It was darkly written upon the face of Aunt Marcia.

Antoinette was still protesting. "This is a very clumsy and embarrassing thing, Aunt Marcia," she said.

"Embarrassing?" said Aunt Marcia. "It is." She turned a gloomy eye upon me. "Young man, you saw that I was talking to Pierre Reynal?"

"I did," I confessed.

"He has told me everything that you will

imagine he could tell, to point out to me that *Monsieur* is not a fit person to become the husband of my niece. May I be forgiven for bringing her to this place and the curse that rests on it. But the curse already seems to be working in Antoinette, because, when I repeated to her what Reynal had told me, she refused to leave the château. Merciful heavens, Antoinette, what is in your mind? What are you thinking of, Toni?"

Antoinette said nothing. She sat by the window with her head turned a little away, as though she were more interested in the loveliness of the day outside than in what might be said in this room. Yet I thought that I saw in her a tenseness that had so bewildered me at the door of Lafitte's room, the same tremulous sense of weakness. Although there was more reason for it now that the revelations that Reynal was capable of making had been poured into her ear.

"You see?" said *Mademoiselle* Marcia to me. "She acts like that. I don't recognize her. How in the name of all that is wonderful has *Monsieur* been able to hypnotize this girl? And now, Jean Limousin, are you willing to answer some of my questions truthfully?"

"I shall say what I can," I tried to assure her.

"Tell me first, then, if it is not true that *Monsieur* has been a haunting ghost to you all the days of your life?"

I turned that blunt question back and forth in my mind. "It is an odd question to ask concerning my father," I replied.

"I can say that by implication you have said yes. But I want something more concrete. Is it not true, Jean, that *Monsieur* on a certain night rose from the dinner table and denounced you and ordered you from his house?"

I was cold and sick to my very soul. "I had transgressed his express commands," I told her.

"But is it true?"

"It is true," I was forced to whisper.

"Ah, you have this confirmation, Toni," announced that terrible *Mademoiselle* Marcia. "Will you look at Jean?"

"Yes," said Antoinette, but she looked upon the floor only as though, I swear, she feared to lift her eyes to mine.

"Will you consider, Toni, that there was never a gentler soul in the world than that of this poor boy?"

"I do consider it," Antoinette replied in a shaken voice.

"And yet he was ordered from his father's house . . . because the foolish child had been tempted to play cards . . . and had lost a few score of dollars. Do you hear me, Toni?"

"I do." She spoke as if the words were wrung from her.

"Toni, is there no sense of pity in you?"

"Oh, yes, Aunt Marcia."

"But that is not all. Is it not true . . . answer me, Jean Limousin, as you hope for heaven . . . that when *Monsieur* was denouncing you, your poor young mother ran in between you and begged him . . . ?"

It lifted me from my chair, to the back of which I clung, wavering. *"Mademoiselle!"* I gasped out.

"Ah, I am sorry, Jean. But for the sake of opening the eyes of this poor child . . . is it not true that he brushed her brutally aside, and that she fell to the floor, Jean?"

I covered my eyes.

"She died, Jean, in your arms, with her last breath begging *Monsieur* to show you mercy. Is it not true?"

I was too dizzy and sick to answer, and I was kept from the need of it by a strange intervention. Antoinette jumped up and cried suddenly: "You shall not speak of it, Jean! You shall not ask him another question, Aunt Marcia. Ah, is there no shame in you? Is there no shame?"

311

"I want truth, Antoinette, you blind girl. I want the truth for yourself, and you must have it. Then tell me, Jean Limousin, if it is not true that *Monsieur* pretended a reconciliation with you, and that he bribed you with money and with your safety from the hand of the law to return to the château and pretend a genuine affection for him? If he did not bribe you to do this in order that the suspicions of Antoinette and of me should be killed? Is not *that* true?"

"Jean," cried Antoinette, "you need not answer . . . you must not answer! I shall close my ears. I shall not hear him, Aunt Marcia!"

She tried to run from the room, but *Mademoiselle* Marcia caught her with an arm as strong as the arm of a man and held her.

"Answer me, miserable boy!" she yelled. "Heaven forgive you for what you have done or tried to do, if you speak the truth to us now. Oh, look, Toni, and see the guilt in his face, even if you will not listen to his voice."

I said in a voice so hoarse that I had to try twice before I could make myself heard: "*Mademoiselle* Marcia, it is all true . . . and less than the truth."

There was a moan from Antoinette, and

she dropped her head on the shoulder of Aunt Marcia.

"I honor you, Jean," Marcia Gerardin said. "Even if it is a late confession, I honor you for it."

"Will you believe me, *Mademoiselle* Marcia?" I said. "I could not have let the marriage take place without speaking . . . but like a wretched coward have delayed from day to day."

"Do you hear, Toni?" said Marcia Gerardin. "Do your hear what Jean has told us? Does it mean anything to you?"

She only murmured: "Let me go, Aunt Marcia. I shall die if you keep me here."

"Will you face Jean and . . . ?"

"Face him? No . . . no . . . no!"

To my astonishment, to the very visible horror of *Mademoiselle* Marcia, Antoinette burst into tears.

"The world is ending!" Marcia lamented to me with a startled look. "Antoinette . . . come!"

And she led her out of the room.

There was a very perceptible time after this, but I had not yet gathered enough strength to leave that torture chamber when *Monsieur* came in to me. He gave me a single look and then accused: "You have talked, baby. You have chattered of everything you know! Is it true?"

"I have told her everything that she asked," I answered. "At least, I have told her what seems to hurt you most."

"How blessed I am in such a son," *Monsieur* murmured. "Ah, what a blessing are children."

He was in such a cold fury that I shrank away from him. I think, if he had stirred a step toward me, that I should have flung myself through the plate glass of the big window; I should have leaped over a cliff to avoid him.

He saw it at once and merely sneered at me. "I am not going to put a hand on you," he said. "For such things as this a mere physical punishment is nothing . . . nothing. But there are other ways of which you will learn. You are not the son of a fool, my dear Jean. You are not the son of a fool, of that you may be sure!"

He was about to say more and find some vent to his agony through his acid tongue when the door was cast open by *Mademoiselle* Marcia. She was as full of fire as *Monsieur* himself.

"I am glad that I have found you together," she said, "and I suppose that you are counting the number of eggs left in the basket. But, in the first place, I shall announce your victory, *Monsieur*. What madness has taken hold on her, I cannot tell, but with her eyes opened to the truth, with all the black facts arrayed before her, she will not see the light."

The voice of *Monsieur* was like a shout of victory. "By all that is noble in heaven!" he cried. "She still will not leave the château!"

"She will not," *Mademoiselle* Marcia attested gloomily. "But I have come to warn you, *Monsieur,* that your victory is not complete. Until the day for this unlucky marriage arrives, I shall be striving my poor best to bring her to her senses. And, in the meantime, I shall wait for you, Jean Limousin, to show that you are worthy of your mother, and not a coward."

With this fierce announcement, she turned her back on us and went from the room, pausing once or twice as though there were many more words in her that she yearned to utter. At last she disappeared through the doorway, and we could follow her heavy step as she went up the hall and then up the stairs.

*Monsieur,* after this bewildering revelation, was a changed man. He was able to sit down and light a cigarette, saying: "I could not have guessed it. Frankly, I should have known that to a nature as proud and as strong as hers, only what comes into her own life affects her will. If she had decided to marry me, what would the revelations of creatures like Reynal and Jean Limousin mean to her? Nothing! She is a goddess, and she must know the gap that extends between her and other women. Yet it is very wonderful. As for love . . . no, I cannot delude myself. It is only esteem. Not for my wealth. She is above that. It is esteem for the mind of *Monsieur*. Oh, strange and wise and beautiful girl!"

He paused in his ecstasy and said dryly to me: "I retract some of what I have spoken to you, Jean. Perhaps it was better that she should have known everything before the marriage. I have sailed my ship between the reefs. There is a fair harbor before me now."

# Chapter
# Thirty-Five

# A Ride on the Gray

There are times when, in an emotional crisis, moments run as slowly as they drag along on a railroad platform when the train is late. What I felt when I left *Monsieur* was a feverish desire to find some employment. If I could have put a canoe into the river and paddled it with all my might, it would have been most to my liking. But, remembering my last trip down the river with my mother in the boat, I shrank from that amusement. A walk would not be motion swift enough for me. By instinct rather than actual desire, I found myself in my room changing my clothes and putting on riding togs.

If I wanted a smooth jaunt over the well-built roads, there were wire-strung Thoroughbreds that would flash me along like the wind, or there was the young mare that

*Monsieur* was using for hacking back and forth on the estate. What I wanted, however, was to plunge through the woods, get into the thick of cross-country action, and pour as much excitement as possible into my moments in the saddle. So I asked McGurdy for the big, gray Irish hunter, and he had the monster brought out.

"He's better in the knees every day," said McGurdy, looking critically from the side. "It would take a wise eye to see that he's broke down. *I* think he'll come back near to shape. Are you meaning some stiff work for him?"

I told him that I felt like a brisk spin across country, the crosser the better, and at this McGurdy looked me in the eye, and said: "I'd lay to it that you'd like the new path, sir."

"The new path, McGurdy?" I questioned him. "Why, man, it's smooth enough for a child to take its first riding lesson on. What fun would there be on the new path?"

*Monsieur* had barely finished the construction of it. It wove among the trees, dipping pleasantly with the rise and drop of the ground, from the château to the riverside. I had been over it once and did not like it — because the cleavage through the trees left them too raw-edged, the gravel was too firmly rolled, and on the whole there was a pioneer air of newness about the path that made me decide to keep off it for another year, at the least.

McGurdy made a gesture with both hands and cocked a deprecatory head upon one side. "You never can tell where the fun will come," he responded. "Sometimes in the rough. Sometimes over the flat. You never can tell where the hardest falls are coming."

"Now what do you mean by that, McGurdy?"

He would only shrug his shoulders and study an aimless diagram that he drew in the gravel with the toe of his boot. "I dunno," he said. "I just gave you a suggestion for a ride. You suit yourself."

With which he strode off toward the stable doors. Of course, no one employed at the château would have dared to use such insolence — no one other than McGurdy, who had made himself so useful to *Monsieur* that I think my father would have parted with his right arm sooner than with this omniscient horseman. I felt that it was strange conduct, even for McGurdy. It looked remarkably as though he felt that the river ride had a mysterious interest for him — and for me.

On this day I was exactly in the mood for riding straight down the throat of the first mystery I could find. The dangers in the château, which lay like a cloud behind me, were such impalpable, shadowy things that I would have welcomed some physical threat. I had a holster strapped to my hip, and I was wickedly prepared to use it, I assure you. So I took the river road, which brought me upon my destiny. Even so I might have gone whisking by my fate, had it not been for a great freak of chance to which I have been grateful ever since. For the gray Irish hunter, so famous for the sureness of his footing, so wise of head and perfect in schooling — this paragon of a hunter who had worked across the worst of rough country with never a misstep stumbled as he ran down that smoothly finished trail and flung me straightway over his head.

I was shooting the big animal along at a racing gait, eager to be off the new path and away though the woods. I was jockeying him with my body pitched along his neck, with so little expectation of any mishap underfoot that heavy stumble flicked me lightly off his back. I landed in thick shrubbery that received me like a set of wonderful springs and tossed me back upon my feet, where I gasped once or twice and then started after the gray. That wise beast, having bolted for half a furlong, now came about and waited patiently for me to catch up with it. It was while I hastened toward it, cursing and stamping, that a familiar shadow glided out of the woods upon my right. I whirled about upon Pierre Reynal.

He was more repulsive in appearance than ever. Under a beard of four or five days, his ugly face was blotched and swollen where the blows of *Monsieur* had fallen during their murderous battle. Although he was leaning on a long rifle, I did not make the least gesture toward my own weapon. If it were true that this Reynal had been my very vindictive enemy during most of my life, and that he had attempted to kill my father not long before, still what can one do to a man who will not strike back? I had learned from experience that this brave and terrible man would not lift his hand against me. I regarded him, therefore, with only a little more than my usual interest and loathing. Some people have such feelings of revulsion when they see a spider crawling or a snake coiling — it was in this manner that I regarded Reynal. I never could keep my emotion about him sufficiently behind a mask. This was almost the first time that he cared to speak of it.

"You are as happy as ever to see me, *Monsieur* Jean," Reynal said.

"I cannot see you," I answered him sternly, "without feeling that it is my duty to shoot you down or call for others to help me."

"Your duty to whom, *monsieur?*"

"For one, to my father, whom you have tried to murder, Reynal."

"But is it murder to stand before a man and to fight with your two hands?"

"I shall not argue. Only, Reynal, if you love your life, do not remain on the grounds of the château long, for *Monsieur* has sent out a dozen men to hunt through the woods for you. And if they find you, they are instructed to say that they mistook you for a rabbit."

Reynal favored me with his frightful smile. "You are too kind, *Monsieur* Jean," he said.

"You knew it all before, Reynal," I said, understanding him at once. "You seem to have your informers. Tell me . . . did you direct McGurdy to send me down this path to you?"

"Is McGurdy a man to be commanded?" asked Reynal, with one of those graceful Latin gestures that were so incongruous in the man.

"Very well," I said. "You may choose to play with this danger, if you will, but I cannot help warning you. In spite of all the reasons I have for hating you, Reynal, I have a kindly feeling toward you. I wish you no harm."

Reynal seemed moved by this, and he even made a step or two toward me, saying: "*Monsieur* Jean, is it true? Is there one touch of fondness in you for Pierre Reynal?"

I could not help shrinking from him, and I said coldly: "I said that I did not hate you, Reynal, and I have no wish to see you lose your life, which you will surely do if you remain near *Monsieur.*"

"It is true," Reynal agreed, standing again. "In fact, this is the last day."

"You are leaving the place, then?"

"I am leaving, *Monsieur* Jean," he said with his ugly smile. "I shall not see you again," he added in a singular voice, "although you may see Pierre Reynal."

"Now, what do you mean by that?" I asked him.

"Forgive me for such a riddle," he said,

"but we have not a great deal of time. The reason that you rode down this new path was to learn something from me that I must tell you now."

"What is that, then?" I asked, very curious, indeed.

"It is the reason why *Mademoiselle* Antoinette Gerardin is remaining at the château," he said.

"And you can tell me that? However, I know it well enough."

"If you know, why are you here? But you do not know, and I will tell you. You dream that it is because the strength and the strangeness of *Monsieur* have surrounded her. Ah, how blind you are, Jean. She remains today and tomorrow and perhaps even more days, almost to the very moment that *Monsieur* has appointed for the marriage, and it is because she has no power to take herself away from the man she loves. What a love it is, Jean, that keeps her chained here, although she dreads and loathes *Monsieur!*"

Now I leaped, with a great, blind flight of the spine, upon his meaning.

"Reynal, Reynal," I cried, "do not taunt and mock me! But you could not know . . . there is no means by which you may be able to know!"

"Is there not?" he asked. "Nevertheless, I have a perfect knowledge of it. It is you whom she loves, Jean. Your arms are the first that were ever around her. Tell me, my dear, blind Jean, is she a woman to whom such a thing could happen by chance? No, no! Go back to her. Go quickly. Only, beware of *Monsieur.* He is already full of many doubts. Beware of *Monsieur.* Go with open eyes, but go at once, because every moment is a torment to her."

I struggled for an instant to understand how it could be. Then I felt that I must not try to reason it out, but do blindly what Reynal had directed, as though he were a prophet sent to me from heaven. I rushed for the gray hunter and sent him hurling back to the château.

When I dismounted at the stables, it was McGurdy himself who took the horse.

"What?" he asked. "Did you find a fall even on a smooth road like that?"

I looked at him wildly and cried: "McGurdy, heaven bless you!"

So I rushed away to the château, leaving McGurdy gaping after me, reasonably sure, I have no doubt, that I was a madman in very fact.

# Chapter
# Thirty-Six

# An Incarnate Devil

I went toward the western entrance of the building, feeling that I was less apt to encounter *Monsieur* if I went in from that direction. He was apt to be in the library at this time of the day, or working in his office. Nothing could happen of a sufficient importance to take him from his work. When I hurried through the garden, I found Antoinette there, dressed in a great stiff apron, with gloves and a huge pair of shears, cutting long-stemmed roses.

Suddenly I felt that the one subject of importance, which everyone pretending to culture should thoroughly master, was flowers. Then again I thanked heaven that I found her dressed in this fashion, so busy, and so plain, like any gardener's wife. It would be easier to talk with her, yes, and to talk privately. The overgrown hedge that bounded this little square of garden shut it off from all of the windows of the château except two tall gables where was that long-unused room of Hubert Guillaume. Even at that moment, with joy leaping in me, I felt as though the eyes of my dead brother had looked down upon me.

Antoinette saw me with a side-glance when I first came near her. I saw her start a little. She pretended that she had not. She was very collected when she straightened from clipping a stem and showed me the bunch she had gathered.

"The garden is going frightfully to pot," said Antoinette.

I looked from the roses to her face, and back to the roses again, without being able to speak a word. Antoinette leaned over suddenly and seemed to busy herself with selecting the next rose. Then I said: "Antoinette, I must talk to you a little."

She did not look up at me. "What do you wish to say, Jean?"

"I wish to say . . . I wish to say . . . do you not despise me for the manner in which I took advantage of you yesterday?"

I thought I saw that her hands stopped fumbling among the tall stems. "No,

Jean," she responded.

"I . . . I can't talk to you, Antoinette . . . unless I can see your face."

"Of course," she said in a rather stifled voice, and began to rise.

In some manner the roses slipped from her arm and tumbled to the ground. I dropped on my knees to pick them up, but I reached only blindly for them, for the face of Antoinette was scant inches from mine, and I could not help seeing that she was flushed a sweeter color than the flowers themselves.

"Antoinette," I said, trembling.

"Yes, Jean. . . ."

"It was not madness that made me. . . . I mean it was the truth, Antoinette."

"I don't understand," she said, rising in great haste. "But I must go back to the house. I have forgotten. . . ."

She left me kneeling foolishly, but it seemed to me that she did not hurry very fast down the path to the house. Once she almost paused. Before she reached the gate, I was in front of her, having trampled the roses to a horrid pulp on my way.

I stammered: "If you leave me, Antoinette . . . if you run away from me in this way . . . I shall not know what to do. I shall go mad."

"But, Jean, I forgot. . . ."

She tried to shrink past me, but I touched her arm, and the touch was enough to stop her. She turned to me, with her eyes down and her lips parted a little. I felt the trembling of her body, and suddenly I knew all that I wished to know — so that a great sense of power made me cruel.

I said: "Will you look up to me, Antoinette? Do you fear to look up to me?"

"Of course not," she said, but it was no more than a whisper, and all that I had was one frightened flash of her eyes. At that I was a madman, indeed.

"Antoinette," I cried, "tell me if God has made me happy . . . tell me if you love me!"

"Do not touch me, Jean," she said. "The house . . . if *Monsieur.* . . ."

"What of him?"

"Would he not kill even his son?"

"I, also, am a Limousin!" I insisted, full of courage. "Do I care if the whole world should see?"

"Jean!" she gasped out. "Do not touch me . . . come no closer, and I shall tell you everything . . . but don't touch me . . . let no one see."

"Tell me, then."

"You will promise? You will not come near me?"

"On my soul."

"Then. . . . Oh, Jean, from the first day I knew! From the first moment that you came to me, I knew that I loved you. But, Jean, you have sworn."

"It is too much happiness. It will kill me," I said. "I only wish to fall on my knees before you, to tell you how I worship you, my beautiful Antoinette."

"You must let me go past you now, Jean. Do not stop me. Do not touch me, or I shall be in your arms, telling you. . . ."

"There is no one to see in those two windows. There is no one."

"I cannot tell, Jean, because there is a mist over my eyes, and I can only see you, oh, my dearest."

"Antoinette. . . ."

"Do not, Jean. Do not touch me."

"I cannot live without one kiss."

"It might be the last. I am afraid! Oh, Jean, be patient, and you shall have me forever as your wife. But now. . . ."

Twice I had taken hold upon myself and drawn myself back, and twice this rosy, trembling beauty called me closer. She was half in fear and half in smiles, and, with every instance, her dark eyes, which looked every way except into mine, were more filled with magic. Against all the power of my will, I held out my arms to her, and she, with a little moan, stepped within them.

Then the lips of Antoinette were saying against my lips: "Am I to die, Jean? Because such wild, sweet, sad happiness must be followed with pain."

"There is no such thing as death," I whispered, "because every hour of our life together will be as unending as . . . what is it?"

She had suddenly shrunk in my arms with a sort of indrawn cry of agony. The sound of the voice was less than the word she spoke, for in that word the terror and the grief and the pain of my life were summed: *"Monsieur!"*

I have never known what brought him there, except that the great emotions of the last two days may have carried into his mind the thoughts of the first *Madame* Limousin and of their dead boy, Hubert Guillaume. When I turned, I knew to look up to the tall gables of the room of my brother. There, somewhat dim behind the glass, like an image in water, I saw *Monsieur.* At that instant, he stepped back into the shadow of the room.

"Antoinette," I said savagely, "you must not faint."

"I shall not. I am perfectly strong. I shall go in to face him, Jean, and. . . ."

Believe me that, as she spoke, she was already moving toward the gate, but I stopped her and swept her back in an ecstasy of fear.

"Face him? You had better face the fiend!" I cried to her. "No, no! We have only one surety for our lives, and that is never to let him find us. He would not pause. My life or yours means nothing to him at this moment."

She fled with me through the garden and beyond, toward the woods.

"The river . . . and the canoe," I panted. "No more talk . . . keep every breath for running."

I dropped back a half pace behind her. She had torn off that clumsy gardener's apron and the big hat and the heavy gloves. Now I watched her running like a boy, with the very wind in her feet.

We flashed down the curve of the broad path that wound into the woods toward the river, leaving the grave of Hubert Guillaume at our right, then through that narrow cleft in the trees that *Monsieur* had opened to give the grave a prospect of the river that Hubert had loved so well. We turned from that to a narrower bridle path, and we were already well down it when I heard the beat of hoofs of a horse, flying at full speed. Antoinette cast one glance of agony toward me and gave her last strength to her running. I saw instantly that it would not do. I took her arm and stopped her.

"We can never reach the water in time," I said.

"Then the trees, Jean. . . ."

"He would hunt us down in five minutes. No, he must meet me here. Go into the woods, Antoinette. Hurry up to the house. I shall stay here and try to persuade him to be reasonable."

She made a first step to obey me, and then whirled back. "You are not armed, Jean?"

"I am not," I said firmly. "But do not think that he will go so far as that. I am his son, after all."

"You have told me yourself that he will be a fiend. And I know that he will. Jean, if you stay to face him. . . ."

She had thrown an arm around me to draw me toward the sheltering trees. As she did so, by an unlucky chance, her hand touched the revolver beneath my coat. It was in her hand instantly.

"You did not mean it!" cried poor Antoinette.

But I was possessed then of the devil that lived in the blood of *Monsieur* himself. I tore the gun from her fingers.

"Go to the house, Antoinette!" I commanded her in a terrible voice. "Find whatever men you can at the château and bring them here. They may not come too late!"

"It is your father!" she said, trying vainly to get the weapon again.

"It is an incarnate devil," I answered her, and brushed her away. "If there is a death, it is on his head. Go back, Antoinette."

Here *Monsieur* broke into our view as he swung his horse from the broader river road and rushed down the path toward us.

# Chapter Thirty-Seven

# Reynal's Secret

To have followed us so quickly, he could not have waited an instant; indeed, he had not paused even to buckle a gun about his hips, but he carried a naked weapon in one hand while he gathered the reins in the other. His head was bare, with the hair he wore so long whipping back and his short beard parted by the wind of that racing gallop. To me, standing on lower ground, he looked like a giant. But I was neither afraid nor too excited. His own blood was rising in me as I held the revolver ready and brushed Antoinette away a second time.

It seemed that God would not give to the earth so terrible a crime, for out from the trees before *Monsieur* stepped Pierre Reynal with one hand raised to warn back my father and a long rifle in the other.

*Monsieur* did not even draw rein, but shot Reynal down and fired again into his body as he rushed past and on toward me.

Afterward, when the wounds were seen, no one could tell how enough life had remained in Reynal to permit him to do the thing, but I saw him twist upon his side and level the rifle. His bullet struck *Monsieur* fairly in the back, and the big man cast up his arms and swayed from the saddle. He rolled to my feet in a cloud of dust and flying gravel, and lay on his face, with a great red stain growing on the back of his coat.

When I turned him on his back again, I thought from his open, fixed eyes that he was already dead, but he said at once in a wonderfully natural voice: "It was Reynal, was it not?"

"It was Reynal," I said.

"There are nine lives in that cat, then," said *Monsieur.*

I was working with stumbling hands to cut away his coat.

"Do not trouble yourself," *Monsieur* said. "I am a dead man. But put me on the grass. I have a foolish aversion to dying like a dog in the dirt."

I did not need to tell Antoinette what to do. She had caught that plunging horse already and dragged herself into the saddle and flown up the road for help. As for *Monsieur,* he was miraculous.

"Have a look at Reynal," he said. "The hero should not be allowed to die without a hand to close his eyes . . . your hand above all, Jean."

I reached Reynal in three bounds, but he was dead long before. Either of the bullets of *Monsieur* would have ended him. I merely paused to lift him from the road and covered his face. Then I hurried back to *Monsieur.*

It did not seem possible that he was dying. The bank to which I had moved the great bulk of his body sloped sharply, so that he might have been thought reclining for a moment to enjoy the strangeness and the beauty of the sky. The mist of the morning had not cleared away with the progress of the day, but was drawing thicker and thicker. It was now a sheet of milky white, luminous with the sun behind, and every green tree stood against this background in unearthly beauty. Even the Limousin River flowed pale between its banks. To complete the illusion, he had lighted a cigarette when I reached him again, although I think that this was rather an affectation, for by the tremor of his hand I guessed that every movement of his arm was a mortal agony to him. I begged him to lie quietly and to allow me to attempt to bandage the wound and stop the flow of death. He merely smiled at me.

"You talk, my boy," he said, "as though I had made a will and as though there were still time for me to change it. You need have no fears. I have no will. The estate passes to you freely. Do not spend it too fast, Jean. Let it linger for a few years."

"*Monsieur,*" I said. "I swear that I wish to receive your commands."

He grunted at this, and then smiled at me his old smile that had chilled my blood so many times in the years before.

"An obedient son, now," *Monsieur* said. "A moment ago, when you stood there waiting for me with a gun in your hand, I could have sworn that the Limousin blood flowed in you, after all. But now will you show weakness? No, Jean, be bold. Talk frankly, because I love frank strength and have always loved it. It will amuse me to hear you tell me now how you hate me."

"*Monsieur,*" I said, "believe that I have forgotten everything except that you are my father. Believe that there was never a time when I could not have loved you if you would have had it so."

"Tush!" he murmured. "Even after Julie?"

I shuddered. "Even after that," I said, and I think that I meant it truly. "But now compose yourself and do not waste your strength talking. There will be a doctor in a few moments. Something still can be done. I am sure of it."

"I detest arguments," *Monsieur* protested. "Let me tell you finally that the ice of death is in me. My body is already dying. My brain will follow soon after. Look at Reynal, though, with his face covered. Well, it is an infinite consolation to know that while he lies there I am enjoying the tender green of these trees . . . and your conversation, my dear Jean."

Once more he smiled on me in his terrible way. It was impossible, even then, to pity him as much as I feared him.

"Is it not a strange day, Jean? And is it not fitting that such a life as mine should close with such a scene? On a miraculous day, and by the hand of my son."

"Not mine!" I cried.

"Don't quibble," *Monsieur* countered. "The hand of Reynal was your hand. He struck for your sake."

"No, no! I have no part in it! Do not say

it, *Monsieur,* or I shall be haunted the rest of my life!"

He looked at me for a moment thoughtfully. "That is the voice of Julie," he said. "And I swear that I believe that you will grieve for me after I am dead, just as she loved me when I was living. Well, I was a mystery to her, poor child, but she was a greater mystery to me. But think of Reynal. Raise him a monument higher than these trees. He saved you, my gentle Jean. For I would surely have laid you where I am now lying. Even if the jury bribes had cost me half my estate. For when I saw you. . . . I cannot think of it. That she should have looked from me down to you. No more of that. We return to Reynal."

"I could never understand him," I said. "Why he should have tormented me, striven to ruin me with you . . . and then. . . ."

"And become your slave the moment you left me? Shall I leave you your little mystery in order that it may dignify your entire life? No, I shall tell you the truth, which is not so marvelous. Well, Jean, when your mother and I were touring in Europe, a certain young, strange Frenchman who was about to take Holy Orders saw your mother. He gave up the divine calling to follow her divine face. That was Pierre Reynal."

"Impossible!" I gasped. "My mother never knew it!"

"Ah, but she did . . . or guessed it. Even Julie was not such a fool. Very well, Jean. He knew that he could not have her. He decided that he would take the creature that looked most like her. You, my dear boy. There is still a bit of the girl look about your face. And the scheme of that madman, that odd Reynal, was simply to disgrace you in my eyes so that you would be forced into the world, where he would make himself necessary to you and become like your father . . . like your slave. I think he hardly cared which."

*Monsieur* laughed softly because of the torment that it caused him. "Very delightful that his ugliness should have driven you almost mad in your childhood. An exquisite irony of fate." He made a sharp pause and closed his eyes; his color had become livid, then settled to a deathly gray.

"It is nearly the end," said *Monsieur*. "I shall not open my eyes again except to behold her for the last time. If Antoinette comes again . . . speak to me . . . but otherwise let me die in peace."

What the doctors will say I do not know, but my own conviction is that my father would have died at that instant except that, by a giant use of his will, he drove death back from him.

He opened his lips to say only one thing: "Faster!" That was the only one thing: "Faster!" That was when the beat of the hoofs of horses and the rolling of the wheels were heard by us from the upper path. Antoinette flew in the lead on *Monsieur*'s tall horse; behind her came a carriage with half a dozen men jumbled in it. Antoinette herself was first. As she slid into my arms, and the horse trotted off, I said: "Go to him."

She went at once and kneeled beside him. *"Monsieur!"* she said.

If I had never guessed that the soul of Antoinette was the purest gold, I should have known it then as I heard the fear, the hatred, the horror banished from her throat, and nothing but the music of tender pity coming to the ears of that dying man.

He looked up at her with eyes wonderfully bright. And he smiled. "How delightful . . . how delightful you are. I fill my eyes with you, and so I am sure that I take you with me into eternity."

All the life that was in him he had saved for that sight of her and for that speech. With the last word the life ran out from that great body, and he was dead without a struggle, without the lifting of a hand, with the smile still on his lips.

This must be the end. I had thought to tell of many other things. Now that I write of how the breath left the lips of *Monsieur,* I see that nothing remains of great importance that you should know, except how we laid *Monsieur* beside Hubert Guillaume. Through my window at this moment I can see the maple leaves sprouting in a delicately beautiful mist of rose above the tomb.

Reynal lies in the little church in the village of Limousin. We placed him where the chanted masses would roll over his grave on every day of the year, because, as we felt then, and as I know now by the sad wisdom which long years give to us, he was a holy man. Tomorrow the carriage will roll to the front of the château, and I shall go out and find a little, withered, white-headed man sitting in it. It will be McGurdy. We will drive together to Limousin and enter the church and sit there together. Hardly a fortnight passes that we do not do it. McGurdy, because he had loved Reynal for reasons that I do not know, drops on his feeble knees and prays. I can only sit and think until my heart swells too much and I must hurry out under the kind sky.

Last of all, of my sweet Antoinette, my dear, my dear wife — but no, I shall not write of this, because I have put down too many words of sorrow, and here I must say farewell.